# So he had rec

'The nurse mentio[...]
and I assumed you[...]

'That's understandable,' he commented in his deep, resonant voice. 'I, on the other hand, had an unfair advantage. I knew your name.'

Natalie stifled a gasp. Expecting the worst, her ears buzzed from nervousness. Did he recognize her?

Instead, he tapped the name-tag on her silk blouse. 'You can't remain anonymous wearing one of these.'

Her hand flew to the pin and she stroked the carved letters before offering a weak chuckle. Her secret was still safe. 'I guess not.'

**Jessica Matthews'** interest in medicine began at a young age, and she nourished it with medical stories and hospital-based television programmes. After a stint as a teenage candy-striper, she pursued a career as a clinical laboratory scientist. When not writing or on duty she fills her day with countless family and school-related activities. Jessica lives in the central United States with her husband, daughter and son.

**Recent titles by the same author:**

THE CALL OF DUTY

# A FRESH
# DIAGNOSIS

BY
JESSICA MATTHEWS

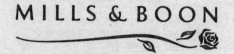

MILLS & BOON

To my children with love, and to Leah, microbiologist
extraordinaire.

*MILLS & BOON, the Rose Device and
LOVE ON CALL are trademarks of the publisher.
Harlequin Mills & Boon Limited,
Eton House, 18-24 Paradise Road, Richmond, Surrey TW9 1SR*

© Jessica Matthews 1995

ISBN 0 263 79465 2

*Set in Times 10 on 12 pt. by
Rowland Phototypesetting Limited
Bury St Edmunds, Suffolk*

03-9602-45254

*Made and printed in Great Britain
Cover illustration by Simon Bishop*

# CHAPTER ONE

'PROMISE you'll behave when you meet Dr Alexander this afternoon,' Karen teased, pulling another rack of Petri plates out of the microbiology incubator. 'No kicking, biting or scratching.'

Natalie Canfield turned her back to the window and the prominent office building across the street. 'Is my lowly assistant implying that I'm prejudiced against the good doctor?' she asked in mock-horror.

'Implying? No,' Karen answered. 'Stating a fact? Yes.'

Natalie shrugged, sinking into a chair in front of the microscope. 'Prejudiced is such an ugly word. How about—?'

'Biased? Close-minded? Intolerant?'

She grinned. 'I'd planned to say cautious. Unlike others around here, I'm not ready to give Gideon Alexander the proverbial red-carpet treatment until I see if he's deserving. You wouldn't like to attend his "Welcome to Rocky Hills and St Mark's" party for me, would you?' she finished on a hopeful note.

Karen shook her head as she picked at a colony with a sterile wire loop. 'Jim specifically asked you to represent the micro lab. The honor's all yours.'

'Remind me to add "uncooperative" to your next evaluation,' Natalie replied without rancor.

'I will.'

Natalie smiled at the unconcerned tone of the younger woman. In spite of their supervisor-employee relationship, Karen had become a close friend during the past several years Natalie had worked at this facility. She appreciated Karen's forthrightness and candor, welcoming it after nearly a lifetime of friends and family telling her what they thought she'd want to hear.

She made a notation on a report form, stuck another slide on the microscope's stage and sighed. 'It won't be easy greeting him with open arms.'

'So don't. Tell him hello, and say it's nice to meet him—or any of those meaningless platitudes we fall back on—then disappear in the crowd. Dr Alexander will be so overwhelmed by the hordes of new faces, he won't notice your absence.'

'True, but it still irritates me that Administration routed the funding for our department's remodeling project to his new offices.'

Karen mimed wiping her brow. 'What a relief you're merely irritated and not upset. As I recall, you broke one of our few wooden stools when you heard the news.'

'It wasn't my fault the rickety old thing collapsed when I moved it,' Natalie protested, replacing the glass slide with another from the waiting row. 'If the fellows holding the purse strings around here had come through on their promises, we'd have bought three good ones six months ago.'

'Just be patient,' her friend advised, pushing one set of culture plates aside to study another. 'We'll get our little hole in the ground remodeled.'

'Sooner than they think, too.'

The dark-haired technician peered over her reading-glasses, her eyes owlish. 'What are you talking about?'

Natalie couldn't hold back a smug grin. 'I've seen the purchase order for our new analyzer. And just where will we put it if we don't renovate this room? We've outgrown our space even without the automated equipment.'

Karen's mouth curved into a huge smile. 'I hadn't thought of that. I guess we know why I'm your assistant instead of vice versa.'

'There are days I'd be happy to trade places, and today is one of them. Now, be honest, wouldn't you rather attend the party?'

'I'm positive. I know how much you enjoy socializing, and I'd hate to deprive you of another opportunity.'

'Yeah, right.' Natalie detested hospital social functions, and avoided those events like a case of cholera. She'd grown up well-acquainted with the politics played between guests, and it rankled with her that situations were affected more by exchanged favors and covert agreements than by ability.

'You know,' Natalie mused, 'I don't begrudge Dr Alexander the new offices—Rocky Hills needs more physicians, and St Mark's has to attract them some way—but I wish our public relations people wouldn't offer everything imaginable and then rob money from other areas of the hospital to accommodate their promises. And after all that, the doctors still don't stay.' She grinned. 'Then again, I wasn't disappointed to see the mediocre ones leave.'

'Bill Burns, the recruiter, does work for quantity rather than quality,' Karen admitted. 'Dr Alexander may surprise us, though. Our new internist is from the University of Colorado, and comes highly recommended.'

Natalie stifled a gasp. *The University of Colorado*? Why hadn't she heard that informative tidbit before?

Warning signals flashed in her mind. Did Rocky Hills' newest physician know her father? If he did. . .

She rubbed her forehead, disregarding the disposable gloves protecting her hands.

Impossible, she decided. Her father specialized in orthopedics, while Gideon Alexander's qualifications were in internal medicine. The two areas were worlds apart. Neither man could possibly know the other.

Satisfied with her logic, she let out a breath and willed her adrenalin down to normal levels.

'According to rumor, Bill considers having recruited him a real coup. Dr Alexander had originally planned to accept Benchwood's offer, then changed his mind.'

'Benchwood Springs? The man passed up an opportunity to live in ski-country for a practice on the dusty plains? I thought you said he was smart,' Natalie scoffed.

'Maybe he hates the mountains. Or is afraid of heights.'

'Get real. If the man considered Benchwood, I doubt he has acrophobia. His wife certainly won't be happy with life in this little burg.'

Karen looked thoughtful. 'I haven't heard anything about a wife. He might not have one.' Then she shrugged. 'Regardless, I'm sure Bill enticed him with perks we'll never imagine—beginning with the building across the street.'

'Money can be a prime motivator,' Natalie agreed. Yet something more than a new office had to have attracted a doctor of his supposed caliber to their small community. Rocky Hills had nothing to brag about except miles of open space. One couldn't even praise the fresh air, since the wind often blew from the northwest, carrying the unmistakable odors of the numerous cattle feedlots and processing plants in the area.

For the first time since she'd heard that Gideon Alexander had joined the medical staff, she wanted to meet him. He sounded too good to be true, and since things like this usually were, she was eager to prove her theory.

She also needed to know if her father had sent him. If so, the phone lines between here and Denver would be smoking with her fury.

Natalie scanned the remainder of the slides before clicking off the microscope. 'If anyone from Happy Hearts Preschool calls, tell them the pinworm preps on this batch were all negative. The sooner they send samples from the other kids, the better.'

'Will do.'

She rose, and a small piece of paper pinned to the bulletin board caught her attention. 'What's the status of this blood culture?'

'If you're talking about the one for Coffman in 414, it's pending,' Karen answered, keeping her attention on her work. 'The ward clerk said to collect the sample at two o'clock unless the guy's fever is down. Since she hasn't called to tell us otherwise, I guess we need to pay the man a visit. I'll go in a few minutes, after I finish this set.'

Natalie stripped off her gloves and washed her hands. 'I'll do it.'

'Doesn't the party start at two?'

'So?'

Karen's head bobbed up like a cork in water, and a broad smile spread across her face. 'Stalling?'

'You're on a roll today, Hillyard.' Without a backward glance Natalie left, carrying her tray of supplies.

Within minutes, she approached the nurses's desk. 'Hi, Angie. How's—?'

'I'm glad you're here,' the nursing supervisor declared without preamble. 'Mr Coffman is critical. We've got to have some answers, and we need them now.'

'I understand your concern. Unfortunately you're forgetting how long a culture takes,' Natalie chided. 'Microbiologists are good, but our bugs grow according to their own time-schedule. What's the problem?'

'Peter Coffman is seventy-eight, has a temp of one hundred and two, an erratic pulse and a heart murmur. We're waiting for an EKG report.'

'Endocarditis?'

Angie nodded.

Natalie clicked her tongue. If she found any bacteria at all in the blood culture, the diagnosis would be confirmed—no other tests required.

The condition—an inflammation of the lining surrounding the heart, sometimes involving the valves—was serious, and complications were numerous. Massive doses of antibiotics—appropriate and timely—were vital to patient survival.

'The ambulance brought him after he collapsed at home. I can't give you more information since Doctor has his chart, but according to Coffman's wife he's been taking oral antibiotics for several weeks.'

Natalie mentally moved him from the acute category to the subacute—where the patient often had a better prognosis. 'I'll call the minute I know something,' she promised. 'But it won't be until tomorrow.'

'If that's the best you can do. . . Dr Larrimore considered transferring Mr Coffman, but since we have an internist now he's called for a consultation before he makes a final decision.'

'Has Dr Alexander been by?' Natalie asked, keeping her voice as even as possible. It would serve no purpose to let her dislike for the newest addition to St Mark's medical community—a man she still hadn't met— become common knowledge. From the moment she'd learned of Gideon Alexander's intent to join the staff, the doctor had complicated her professional life. She didn't need—or want—gossip adding fuel to the situation.

Angie shrugged. 'I just got back from lunch and no one said anything.'

Too busy being wined and dined, no doubt. Natalie pushed the uncharitable thought out of her mind. 'Is it okay if I get the lab's samples now? I'm a few minutes early.'

Angie glanced down the hall. 'Go ahead. Doctor was visiting with the family, but the door's open so it should be okay.'

Natalie walked into Coffman's room. Angie's description hit on target—to all outward appearances the man in the bed looked dead. Only the loud blip coming from the heart monitor spoke otherwise. Her nose picked up the distinctive sickroom odor, common to the seriously ill.

Expecting to see the paunchy, fifty-something Robert Larrimore, she was surprised to find a tall man in his mid-thirties standing next to the bed. Without taking time to search for a family resemblance, she guessed him to be Coffman's son.

'If the sight of blood bothers you, you might wait in the hallway. I'll only be a few minutes,' she said, tilting her head up to address the fellow. Unintimidated by his height—a head taller than her own five feet eight—she met and held his dark-eyed gaze without flinching.

She didn't care how successful he looked in his heather-gray pinstripe suit with his nutmeg-brown hair combed to perfection. A glimpse of blood or even a needle brought many men—including macho athletes—literally to their knees; she'd proven that fact a week ago. Her day was too busy to waste precious time completing another pile of accident forms.

The man's rugged face—complete with a nose sporting a bump near the bridge—stayed impassive. After a pregnant pause, he remarked, 'I think I can handle it.' His voice reminded her of a disc jockey's, having the same deep, musical quality that would keep people listening hour after hour.

Natalie hesitated. His set jaw suggested determination, but she had no idea if he spoke the truth or simply refused to give in to a personal weakness.

Shrugging her acceptance, she tore open packages of alcohol wipes, disinfectant swabs and antimicrobial soap sponges with brisk motions. Having an audience had never bothered her before, but today she felt uncomfortable and oddly vulnerable under the intense gaze of the stranger.

She arranged her materials in the order of use. After everything lay in readiness she began the lengthy process of cleansing the skin while explaining the steps to her patient.

'The blood culture I'm taking will help us determine the cause of your fever. Since I don't want to pick up any bacteria normally living on the skin, I'm scrubbing this same spot with several different solutions.'

Peter Coffman might not have been coherent enough to listen, but she'd made it a habit long ago, after a sweet old lady had thanked her for the information. Out of the corner of one eye, she noticed that his son paid close attention.

A few minutes later, she inserted the needle into the vein and filled the vials and bottles she needed. As she began to load her materials onto her tray, he spoke.

'When will you call in a report?' the man asked. 'At least I assume you won't wait for the paper to trail its way to the nurses' station?'

Sympathizing with the man's impatience—waiting was the hardest part of a loved one's illness—Natalie took no offense at the remark. 'Most of the lab results will be available to the doctor within the hour, but the culture will take longer. Probably close to twenty-four.'

'That long?'

'I'm afraid so.' Natalie wished it were possible to speed things along, but bacterial growth couldn't be rushed—microbes adhered to their own timetable. Nor did she consider it appropriate to explain how monetary limitations kept her from using techniques designed to shave off a few hours. It wouldn't be ethical to undermine a client's confidence in a medical facility.

'Thanks,' he replied, his curt answer sounding like a dismissal. Natalie obliged and left the room.

Striding into the microbiology lab, she found Karen swabbing new media plates with the most recent specimens.

'You know,' she began as she prepared a slide with a drop of Coffman's blood, 'my Aunt Harriet insisted plants grew best when she took time to talk to them. Do you suppose our bacteria would respond the same way?' She steeled her face to hide the grin threatening to burst across her face.

Karen lowered the plates in her hands and blinked. 'I think you've been working too many late nights, my dear. Talking to our bugs? Good heavens, they'll put us both on the psychiatric wing.'

Natalie's mirth bubbled out. 'I agree. But it's a thought, isn't it?'

Karen grinned. 'What brought that pearl of wisdom to mind?'

Natalie relayed her conversation in Coffman's room while she stained the now dry slide with chemicals designed to reveal bacteria. Although it was uncommon to detect the microbes on a smear prior to several hours of incubation, she obeyed the physician's request. Exceptions occurred when least expected, and if this was one of those times the quicker she found and identified the microscopic culprit, the sooner Coffman's treatment could begin.

'I can see the medical journals now,' Natalie joked. 'SCIENTIFIC STUDY AT COLORADO HOSPITAL PROVES TALKING TO BACTERIA ACCELERATES GROWTH-RATE.'

'Sounds more like a headline from the gossip rags at the checkout counters. Yup, the stress is finally getting to you,' Karen teased.

'Don't forget—laughter is the best medicine.' Natalie knew its power from personal experience. Without it, she'd never have survived her childhood difficulties.

She placed the slide under the microscope and began her search for structures resembling bacteria, yeast or a fungus.

'Find anything?' Karen asked several minutes later.

'No, but I'll repeat it in a couple of hours.' She

wiped the oil off the slide before glancing at her watch. 'It's three-thirty. I'd better go and pay my respects before the reception ends at four.'

'Don't sound so sad,' Karen replied. 'It's a party, not a wake. Have fun, but don't eat all the chocolate chip cookies—I know how weak your willpower is when they're around.'

'Thanks for watching my weight, Miss Thin-and-Trim. For your information, the swim team meets tonight, so I can afford to eat an extra one.'

'Hey, boss—' Karen exaggerated a pleading note '—if I work hard while you're gone, will you sneak one away for me?'

'As much as there is to do, I'll snitch two.'

Natalie shrugged off her white lab coat and washed her hands. After reaffixing her name-tag onto her rose-colored silk shirt, and straightening the collar with its cross-stitched roses, she patted her curls—courtesy of Shear Styles, Inc—into place. She caught herself tugging on the hair over her ears, knowing that vanity had created the old habit she was still trying to break.

With brisk steps she traveled the hallways, turning down one, then another, in order to reach the cafeteria. Once there, she stopped and stared at the colored balloons decorating the doorframe.

'Looks like we went all out,' Natalie remarked to a familiar staff member leaving the party.

'No kidding. You should see the spread inside,' replied Kathy Arnold from Respiratory Therapy Services. 'And you should see Dr Alexander. . . .' She placed a hand over her heart. 'If he doesn't fill his patient load by the end of his first week, I'll swallow my stethoscope.'

Another fan. 'Handsome, I suppose?' Natalie

smiled, knowing Kathy's tastes weren't exactly discriminatory.

'Charming, too.'

Handsome *and* charming. What a combination.

Taking a deep breath, Natalie stepped over the threshold. Staff members packed the huge cafeteria, and the dull roar of voices filled the air. A familiar wave of insecurity rolled over her, just as it had during her teenage years, when she hadn't been able to hear her companions over the din.

Reminding herself that those days were gone, thanks to modern technology, she squeezed her way to the refreshment table, certain she'd find the guest of honor nearby.

He was.

Her mouth gaped open and she snapped it closed.

The man who had been visiting Peter Coffman hadn't been his son; he'd been his consulting physician.

And she'd asked if the sight of blood bothered him.

Heat crawled up her neck and spread across her face. Thank goodness she hadn't forced him to leave the room.

After a few cleansing breaths her chagrin faded and indignation took its place. Why hadn't he introduced himself? He'd had ample opportunity. How was she, or anyone else for that matter, to know he had earned the right to use the lofty title of 'Doctor'?

Determined to discharge her obligation as soon as possible, she followed a group of three pharmacists to the end of the receiving line. With each step she compared Dr Alexander in a social setting to Dr Alexander in his professional capacity.

His physical appearance and coloring remained the same, but his attitude had changed. A pleasant expression now softened his features, and a small dimple appeared in his left cheek whenever his mouth relaxed into a teeth-baring smile. He looked younger and more approachable than the man she'd observed a few short hours ago.

Hating to admit it, Natalie agreed with Kathy's opinion—Gideon Alexander looked like a model straight from the pages of *Gentlemen's Quarterly*.

Familiar with her father's expensive wardrobe, she judged Alexander's suit as ready-to-wear rather than custom-made apparel—though it was made of good quality material. Regardless, his broad shoulders and long, lean legs filled out the gray pinstripe fabric perfectly.

Her misgivings grew with every advancement in the line. She felt like a hypocrite—welcoming him to the hospital when she resented him for building his practice at her department's expense. Although she wanted to walk away and not look back, a compelling need to discover if he had any ties to her famous father over-ruled the urge. One way or another, she had to learn if he knew Harrison Pike.

She'd come to St Mark's in Rocky Hills two years ago, to succeed on her own merits and without her father's influence. The right word uttered at the wrong time would change people's attitudes overnight. Medical personnel would treat her as the legendary Dr Pike's daughter, not as Natalie Canfield. And at the same time they'd hide their true feelings and opinions in order either to get or remain in her parent's good graces. It happened with amazing regularity.

Pasting what she hoped was a warm smile on her face, she waited her turn. A minute later she stood in front of a man she'd disliked for several months, sight unseen, and her hand found its way into his.

Edward Higgins, the business administrator, who was a stickler for protocol, took his job seriously and performed the introductions. 'Dr Alexander has a special interest in infectious disease, so you two have a lot in common. Since you're in good company, Gideon, will you excuse me for a few minutes?' Without waiting for a reply, he clapped the younger man on the back and strode away.

Ignoring the heat flashing up her arm, Natalie tried not to fidget under the honored guest's scrutiny. His coal-dark eyes gave slow perusal, giving the unmistakable impression that few things escaped his notice. Expecting the same congeniality he'd offered everyone before her, her own smile faltered when his mouth remained in a hard line. For some reason the inscrutable man she'd seen in Coffman's room had returned.

In spite of his cool reception his hand felt warm, and twice the size of hers. 'I'd heard you'd been called for a consult on Mr Coffman,' she stated, breaking the contact. Her skin continued to tingle from the pressure of his lean fingers against hers.

'You caught me on my first official case at St Mark's.'

So he had recognized her, too. 'I wouldn't have interrupted if I'd known you were in the room,' she defended.

'Are you proposing we set out "Doctor at Work" signs, like the road crews use during highway construction?'

Heat rose to her face. 'Not at all,' she replied, matching his arctic-air tone and wondering how anyone could consider him charming. He was obviously enjoying a joke at her expense.

'The nurse mentioned she'd seen the family and I assumed you were one of the relatives.'

'That's understandable,' he commented in his deep, resonant voice. 'I, on the other hand, had an unfair advantage. I knew your name.'

Natalie stifled a gasp. She was expecting the worst, and her ears buzzed from nervousness. Did he recognize her?

Instead, he tapped the name-tag on her silk blouse. 'You can't remain anonymous wearing one of these.'

Her hand flew to the pin, and she stroked the carved letters before offering a weak chuckle. Her secret was still safe. 'I guess not.'

Though she wished for a speedy exit, her mission kept her feet rooted to the spot. Higgins' absence was fortuitous, but she couldn't ask point-blank if Alexander knew Harrison Pike. If he didn't she'd have to offer more explanations than she wanted, and if her father *had* sent him he wouldn't admit it. She'd have to wait and watch—actions spoke louder than words.

'Have you found anything on Coffman yet?' he asked.

'No, but that's not unusual.' His impatience raised her ire. 'I thought all medical students learned that cultures require at least twenty-four hours.'

'That's basic information. However, our lab gave preliminary blood culture reports in eight.'

The news didn't surprise her. 'Unfortunately I don't have the equipment. Twenty-four is the best I can do.'

'Let's hope your best is good enough.'

Natalie took a deep breath. The man was insufferable. 'Surely you've started treatment?'

He nodded, his face grave. 'One of the newer penicillins. That may change, depending on the organism and its response to the antibiotic.'

She phrased her next statement as a question. 'You're certain the cause is bacterial?'

He arched one eyebrow. 'An educated guess.'

'Have you guessed its identity, too? Maybe you don't need my report after all.'

A lazy grin tugged on his mouth—the first smile directed at her. 'Oh, I'll need your report—no doubt about it. In the meantime, I'll assume it's a staph or a streptococcus, since they are the most common culprits.'

For some inexplicable reason, his confidence grated on her. 'Maybe I'll isolate something different,' she commented, crossing her arms.

'As long as you find *something*, Ms Canfield.'

His emphasis seemed like a dare—a dare that for once in her life she readily accepted. 'Don't worry, Doctor. I will.'

Gideon stared into light brown eyes, watching the gold and green flecks sparkle with challenge. Mesmerized by Natalie's long lashes, he inwardly railed at the vagaries of fate.

He had spent all summer convincing himself that Rocky Hills, Colorado, was a fine place to begin a practice. After intense haggling he'd negotiated an office—complete with the latest equipment, a receptionist, billing clerk and nurse—as part of his contract. The hospital had also agreed to pay part of his malpractice insurance premiums. In addition, he'd found a small house within walking distance of the high school, which suited both him and his younger sister.

Unfortunately, ever since he'd seen Natalie Canfield

Pike for the first time in Peter Coffman's room, he'd realized he'd only been fooling himself. He wouldn't have been in this town if it hadn't been for her and her meddling, controlling parent.

But taking his frustration out on her would only create more problems in the long run—not to mention being unprofessional. His plan—his directive, actually—couldn't proceed if sparks flew every time they spoke to each other.

Resolving to shelve his animosity for the time being, he turned to the free-standing punch fountain. 'Would you like some lemonade?'

She blinked, her eyes appearing too large for her face. 'Well. . .sure. . .why not?'

Handing her a small glass, he held his under one of the six streams arcing out of the center column into the stainless steel basin. As soon as she had filled hers, he raised his cup. 'To the future.'

'To the future,' she echoed, obviously puzzled by his abrupt change in attitude.

Sipping the tart beverage, he studied his companion. She was tall for a woman—a bonus in his opinion—but then her father was tall, too.

Her hair, a common shade of brown, was a mass of curls ending below her earlobes. The style fit her oval-shaped face, with its high cheekbones and turned-up nose.

Pike had assessed his twenty-eight-year-old daughter correctly, Gideon decided. From the way she alternated between nervousness and outspokenness, it seemed she didn't know how to play the hospital politics game.

Then again, his verbal sparring didn't speak much for his own skills. The famous Dr Pike should have procured someone else to keep a watchful eye on Natalie's interests.

'Does it always rain this much?' he asked, trying to make small talk.

'No. The old-timers claim that we're in a once-every-fifty-year wet cycle. I don't mind the cloudy days, but I prefer to see the sun.' She changed the subject. 'I understand you could have chosen anywhere in the state to begin a practice.'

He shrugged, then swallowed the last ounces of lemonade in his cup. 'You shouldn't believe everything you hear.'

'Did you really turn down Benchwood Springs?'

He'd seen the same disbelief before; not many people understood why he had chosen a town surrounded by sagebrush and cattle over a growing new ski resort. 'Yes.'

'Why? When I see what this community has to offer, I'm curious as to what brought you here.'

Gideon clenched onto his glass. He couldn't possibly explain that he was a victim of extortion.

All because of her.

# CHAPTER TWO

'ARE you a native?' Gideon refilled his glass and gulped half of its contents.

Too late, Natalie realized she had fallen into his trap. 'No.'

'Then why did *you* move here?'

She hesitated. 'It seemed like a nice place to work.'

'I rest my case.'

Natalie shook her head. 'I can't believe you passed up an opportunity to live in Benchwood Springs.'

'Rocky Hills made a good offer.'

The light dawned. 'So you're here for the money.'

'I didn't say that,' he corrected her, his voice even. 'Coming to St Mark's allowed for career opportunities I wouldn't have received anyplace else.'

Before she could puzzle out his meaning, he continued. 'Yes, the financial aspect was important. Medical school is expensive, and I wasn't born into a family with money or prestige. My father drove a truck and my mother worked as a housekeeper at a local motel. Their income barely covered our family's expenses.'

She gave him a few points for honesty. If he'd confessed to a purely altruistic motive, she'd have laughed in his face. 'You've accomplished so much on your own. I'll bet your parents are proud.'

Gideon swirled the last swallow of lemonade in his cup before he drank it. 'My mom was thrilled. My dad died right after my sister was born.'

'I'm sorry. Where does your mother live?'

'Leadville. She died this summer, in June.'

Pain filled his voice and his eyes turned as bleak as a winter sky. She placed a hand on his arm with a featherlight touch. 'Does the rest of your family live there?'

'My brother and his wife own an architectural firm in Grand Junction. My sister moved with me. By the way, I understand my office building is close to your lab.'

Her spine stiffened. She stepped back and thrust her hands into her pockets. For a few minutes she'd forgotten her budget problems and the part he'd played in them, but his benign comment had reminded her. 'Right across the street.'

'I don't recall seeing any culture supplies on the shelf,' he mentioned more to himself than to her. 'Has my nurse Becky picked them up yet?'

'I don't think so.'

He looked thoughtful. 'If I didn't have a medical staff meeting shortly, I'd get them now. I'd like to visit your lab.'

'There isn't much to see,' she warned him, considering her words an understatement.

'Maybe not. I'd like to anyway.'

Suppressing a resigned sigh, she fixed a smile on her face. 'We're open from six a.m. to six p.m.' As an afterthought, she added, 'Come whenever you like.'

The next morning, Gideon meandered through his offices, checking each cubicle a final time before his first patients arrived. Instruments, gloves, gowns, suturing kits, bandages and every supply imaginable lined the drawers and shelves, waiting to be used.

Stainless steel surfaces gleamed, the floors sparkled, and the fresh, clean scent of soap mingled with the pungent aroma of alcohol. He was ready; the moment he'd been working toward for years had finally arrived—the moment he'd established his own practice.

Suddenly remembering his shortage of lab items, he checked his watch. *Damn.* He couldn't leave now; his first appointment was in ten minutes.

Hating to be caught ill-prepared, he found his nurse in the corridor. 'Becky, would you send someone after my culture supplies? Have them ask for Natalie.'

'Will do.'

While Becky disappeared in search of an available person Gideon visualized the microbiologist. Natalie Canfield Pike would never know how she'd complicated his life.

Wandering into another exam room, he polished a dull spot on the stainless steel floor-lamp with his white coat's sleeve and remembered a warm April morning four short months ago. April sixth, to be exact.

It had begun as an ordinary day—if any day in the life of a busy resident could be considered ordinary. At least it had been ordinary until he'd received a request to see Harrison Pike, Chairman of the University of Colorado's Orthopedics Department, delivered personally by his formidable secretary, Hildreth.

Having met the man once after a lecture, and knowing him only by reputation, Gideon had been both confused and curious. Why was Dr Pike interested in *him*? He'd dug his threadbare tie out of his locker and answered the summons. The fifty-eight-year-old Dr Pike had seemed so friendly and personable, even while he'd dropped his bombshell. . .

\*     \*     \*

'I took the liberty of accepting Rocky Hills' offer on your behalf,' Pike said, looking like a man without a care in the world, with his arm resting on the back of his brushed velour office sofa.

Gideon drew a sharp breath and stared at the physician, whose gun-metal-gray hair added to his distinguished appearance. Thinking his recent inner ear infection had affected his hearing, he tugged on his left ear to equalize the pressure. 'I beg your pardon?'

'I told the Rocky Hills' recruiter you would accept their terms.' Pike's light brown gaze was steady.

A knot of bile rose in Gideon's throat and he swallowed hard. Twice. Instinct commanded him to unleash his fury and dismay; the rules for dealing with medical superiors stressed self-control and respect.

'Why?' he demanded, his voice harsh. With his hackles rising, he clenched his jaw until it ached. World-famous surgeon or not, Pike had no business controlling or interfering with Gideon's life—especially since he studied internal medicine, not orthopedics. He fought the urge to pace, planting his feet on the lush beige carpeting instead.

'I heard you'd narrowed your choices to Benchwood and Rocky Hills.'

'I visited with their representatives on several occasions,' Gideon corrected. 'Listening to their sales pitch hardly constitutes serious consideration. To be truthful, the Rocky Hills recruiter refused to take no for an answer, even though I'd decided against them.'

Pike looked thoughtful and nodded. 'I've done some checking. Benchwood's offer is very attractive; they'll provide a new office and new equipment, pay your malpractice insurance plus guarantee an annual salary.

Then there's the intangible benefits—the mountain scenery, winter skiing, hiking, etcetera, etcetera. Compared to what Rocky Hills will provide, I'd make the same decision.'

Gideon leaned forward. 'Then why—?'

Pike continued as if he hadn't interrupted. 'I have a proposition for you. Cancel your appointment with Benchwood's fellow and meet with Bill Burns, the Rocky Hills representative, instead.'

Hildreth's urgency when she had delivered the summons now made sense. In two short hours he had planned to accept Benchwood's offer—an offer that anyone with intelligence wouldn't refuse, an offer that Rocky Hills couldn't duplicate in any way, shape, or form.

Dr Pike brushed at a fleck of lint on his navy blue pant-leg. 'Rocky Hills has only my verbal commitment, which technically isn't binding. However, if you'll agree to relocate to Rocky Hills, I'll personally make up the difference between their offers.'

Gideon's jaw dropped, and he snapped it closed. The figure he had already calculated—the figure that had played a major role in his decision—popped into his head. 'You do realize how much money we're talking about?'

Pike didn't bat an eye, although the corners of his mouth twitched. 'I do.'

Gideon sank back in the overstuffed cushions. The situation suddenly wasn't as grim as he'd first thought. He wasn't legally bound by Pike's acceptance; he could still make his own choices. He hadn't lost his hold on the controlling reins of his life as he'd feared.

He relaxed, stretching his arm along the top of the sofa. 'Why me?'

'Rocky Hills needs a good internal medicine special-ist. Dr Allen, your department head, recommends you highly. You're the best of all his residents.'

Gideon let Pike's compliment slip by. 'Why Rocky Hills? Other areas of Colorado need internists. Benchwood Springs, for example.' He found himself enjoying the role of devil's advocate. There was more to this situation than what Pike had divulged—both logic and the feeling in the pit of his stomach said so.

'Sentimental reasons.'

Gideon suppressed a cynical laugh. Pike hardly seemed the emotional type. 'A six-digit figure is a high price for sentiment.' He would normally never, ever have spoken so bluntly with a superior, but the code of etiquette he'd obeyed for years didn't apply in these circumstances.

Pike pursed his lips, as if he had difficulty voicing his thoughts. 'My daughter, Natalie, is a microbiologist at St Mark's Hospital in Rocky Hills. She wanted to work in a facility where she was judged on her own merits rather than her name.'

Gideon blinked. Most people he'd encountered in his thirty-two years had capitalized on any and every advantage they could. 'She's to be commended,' he remarked, testing the elder physician's response.

'Oh, definitely. She's a sweet, intelligent young woman, but she hasn't learned how to play hospital politics. Natalie has had a lot of disappointments in her life, and, as a parent, I want to minimize them when I can. Unfortunately, she won't let me.'

'You want me to do it for you?' Gideon guessed.

Dr Pike looked relieved. 'Yes. You'll need to guide her through any rough spots that surface. Since your main interest is in infectious disease, you'll be able to help without raising her suspicion.'

Gideon shook his head. 'You don't want a physician, you want a guardian angel. In case you haven't noticed, my name isn't Gabriel.'

'True, but your namesake was a hero.'

Gideon chose not to divulge how he came to have his name . . . 'I'm not hero material, and I hate playing hospital politics.'

'Who doesn't? Yet, there are times when it is necessary.'

Gideon tried again. 'Look, I'm sure if I ever have a daughter I'll be protective, too. However, I happen to agree with her. A man's—or woman's—success should depend on ability, not on who they are or who they know. You've got the wrong man for this job.' He rose and turned toward the door.

'Dr Allen told me a lot about you. He'll be pleased to learn he was right—money won't entice you into doing something you don't want to do.'

Gideon paused, his brief hesitation the only acknowledgement of Pike's calmly delivered remark. He took another step.

Pike continued. 'If you'd been serious about Rocky Hills, I would have approached you by asking for a simple favor. However, since you leaned toward another facility, I had to change my plan. I wondered what would persuade a dedicated young doctor with an extremely promising future to consider my proposal. Then I had my answer.'

Gideon froze, his breathing suspended. The easy, in-control feeling inside of him had evaporated, and a hard knot of apprehension filled his chest. He faced Pike with his arms at his side, fists clenched and shoulders squared.

Still seated, Pike wore the expression of a man who knew he held a winning poker hand. 'You want to become board-certified in the infectious disease specialty. You also have a position with the Centers for Disease Control or the World Health Organization in your sights as well.'

Gideon gritted his teeth. He didn't know which angered him more—the coercion or the extremely thorough personal investigation.

'Of course,' Dr Pike continued, inspecting his fingernails, 'you'd have to be accepted into a training program first. I'd hate for you to be one of the many whose applications are rejected.' He turned his gaze to Gideon.

Cold sweat trickled down Gideon's neck at the surgeon's thinly veiled threat. He might have known that Dr Pike would do everything possible to get what *he* wanted, regardless of anyone else's wishes or feelings.

'I'm not asking you to do something illegal,' Pike told him. 'Nor am I asking you to relocate to someplace utterly distasteful.'

That's a matter of opinion, Gideon thought. Exchanging a practice in the mountains for one on the dry, flat plains of eastern Colorado wouldn't be a move to garner the envy of his peers or his family.

'Consider my request as a basic exchange of favors—everyone gets what they want.'

'I seem to have more at stake than you do,' Gideon reminded him.

Harrison shrugged. 'Are you willing to work a few years in Rocky Hills instead of Benchwood Springs to ensure your career?'

Gideon rubbed the back of his neck and grimaced. For longer than he could remember he'd dreamed, planned and worked for the opportunity to seek his own destiny. Now he had to change everything so he could nursemaid a spoiled rich kid.

On the other hand, if he didn't agree, Dr Pike would have no qualms about following through on his threat. The surgeon was one of the few physicians famous enough to have clout anywhere in the country.

Yet Gideon couldn't give in so easily. 'I'll be busy with my practice. I won't have time to hold your daughter's hand, and I don't have the inclination to be a counselor,' Gideon ground out.

Pike remained silent.

Gideon strode toward the sofa, his feet making dull thuds on the lush carpeting. 'What makes you think my opinions will carry any weight? I'll be the new man in town, the one fresh out of residency—remember?'

He warmed to his subject. 'What if she has a hare-brained idea? Something totally ridiculous that doesn't have a ghost of a chance with the powers-that-be?'

'Then I'll expect you to show her the error of her ways,' Pike replied matter-of-factly.

Gideon noticed the smile tugging on Pike's mouth. He felt like a mouse in a maze—trapped, with only one way to get out. Pike knew that he knew it, too.

The perfect knot in his navy blue tie tightened, making his collar feel like a hangman's noose. Running his finger along the inside of the fabric to loosen the choke-hold on his trachea, he let out a deep breath.

'What if I don't comply once I'm there?'

The older man grinned, his eyes crinkling at the corners. 'You will because you're a man of integrity.' He leaned forward. 'My daughter is trying to prove something. It's important to her—and to me—that she succeed.'

'Interfering defeats the purpose,' Gideon pointed out. 'Shouldn't she accomplish her goal on her own?'

'She's overcome a lot of obstacles in her life. I simply want to have someone looking out for her.'

Gideon bit the inside of his mouth to hold back a sarcastic remark. He couldn't imagine any hurdle that money wouldn't eliminate.

Before he could ask the older physician to elaborate, the chairman withdrew an envelope from the breast pocket of his suit coat. 'Here's a check for the difference.'

Gideon stared at the white paper. Somehow it seemed underhanded, and similar to bribery. If he accepted the money he'd no longer be his own man; Harrison Pike would own him. The thought left a horrible taste in his mouth, and made him feel as grimy as if he'd just finished a hectic sixteen-hour shift.

No, he didn't want the man to have any more of a hold over him than necessary—even if it meant going deeper in debt. He'd simply have to negotiate a few more concessions from Bill Burns.

'I don't want your money,' he replied, unable to keep his upper lip from curling with distaste. 'However, I *do* want some assurance that you'll honor this so-called agreement. I'm a physician, not a miracle-worker.'

Pike tossed the envelope on the coffee-table. Crossing the room, he grabbed a folder lying on his massive mahogany desk. Passing it to Gideon, he said, 'This letter of recommendation is already in my safe. You may keep this unsigned copy as proof, and you will receive the original when your contract ends. If anything should happen to me before then, my lawyer will date it appropriately.'

'Let me see if I understand this. You want me to—'

'Be her mentor,' Harrison finished. 'That's all.'

'Why not ask someone already on staff?'

For the first time Pike looked uncomfortable. 'My daughter worked at this hospital for six months before she told us where she'd moved. If I contacted a local person now. . .' His voice trailed off. 'That's why you're perfect.'

'You've thought of everything.' Gideon hated the bitterness in his voice, but couldn't help it. The rich and famous always had control.

'I tried to.' Pike cocked his head. 'It won't be as difficult a job as you imagine. My daughter is a smart woman.'

Gideon jumped on the opening. 'Then why me—or anyone else for that matter?'

Pike shrugged. 'Insurance. People buy insurance to cover unforeseen problems—fire, disease, theft, etcetera. I'm simply providing some for my daughter.'

Yeah, right, Gideon thought. 'What if she refuses my help? Maybe she doesn't want an adviser.'

'To coin a phrase, "where there's a will, there's a way". I'm sure you'll manage to convince her it would be in her best interest.'

Gideon mentally added 'stubborn' to her character profile.

'By the way, my daughter can't learn about this conversation under any circumstances,' Pike emphasized. 'Nor can anyone else. It must remain strictly confidential. If Natalie even suspects that I've interfered. . .' His brow wrinkled like a thundercloud, the threat obvious.

'I understand,' Gideon replied, feeling as if a block of cement had been chained to his neck.

'Then you accept my terms?'

Gideon hesitated, his mouth pressed into a hard line. He moved to the window and crossed his arms. A chilling wave of indecision washed through him, turning his skin cold. From the five-storey height he watched automobiles the size of toys move along the street, the noise muted by distance and insulated walls. In the background, blue clouds swirled around white-capped mountains.

The railroad clock hanging across the room ticked away, each tick reminding him that Pike was waiting. De-cide, de-cide, de-cide, the timepiece told him.

Gideon cleared his throat. His one-word reply came out hoarse. 'Yes.'

Pike approached him and clasped his shoulder. 'Then I wish you luck with your practice. . . .'

Gideon broke out of his reverie, remembering how he'd stared at Pike's outstretched palm. Instead of sealing the unholy arrangement with a handshake, he'd dug his hands deep into his lab coat pockets. Pike had had to satisfy himself with Gideon's verbal acceptance; shaking hands would have implied a mutual satisfaction, an agreeable compromise, and none of those conditions had applied.

Realizing he'd duplicated his clenched fists, he relaxed and breathed in the smell of his surroundings. The odor of hospital-strength disinfectant pushed away the memory of lemon furniture polish and Pike's minty aftershave.

From April to August, during his mother's final illness and in those odd moments when he'd taken a break from studying for his internal medicine board exam, he'd conjured up a picture of Natalie Pike.

Depending on his mood, she had ranged from a shy, soft-spoken female, lacking all manner of social skills, to the Wicked Witch of the West, complete with a wart on her crooked, oversized nose and a cackling laugh.

She didn't fit either of those descriptions.

In fact, she was one of the few women he'd met who didn't appear intimidated or awed by his credentials. Ever since he'd announced his plans for medical school, he'd encountered two types of feminine reaction. He was either sized up as a free meal ticket or treated as if he were royalty. Regardless, the simpering and fawning were not responses he enjoyed or appreciated. Natalie's irreverence was an invigorating change.

If any other woman had possessed those same traits, he'd have been delighted. Natalie Pike, however, was forbidden territory. Although she couldn't choose her relatives, having Harrison Pike as her father was a definite drawback. A personal and intimate involvement with this particular female posed too many risks. The price of discovery was too high; he wouldn't gamble his future.

Knowing too much about her and her family could easily have tipped her off, so he'd refused Pike's condensed version of Natalie's life. He'd only learned the name she was currently using—her mother's maiden name.

He berated himself for being more brusque toward her than necessary, but in the future he wouldn't make the same mistake. Already he felt like a double agent, immersed in a cloak-and-dagger operation, and he didn't like it.

His biggest surprise had been her reluctance when he'd asked to visit her lab. Most support staff loved to show off their departments, taking advantage of every opportunity to improve public relations. Success often depended upon building a good image.

With a sinking heart, he realized that this part-time guardian angel business could easily become a full-time job.

'Dr Alexander? Mr Carpenter is here. Room one,' Becky announced from the doorway.

Gideon took the chart she handed him and flicked it open. Glancing through the medical questionnaire required of all new patients, he ambled down the hall.

'What can I do for you today?' he asked, entering the cubicle.

Carpenter, a man in his late forties, with a face as weatherbeaten as his jeans, sat on the exam table. 'I think I got arthritis, Doc. My joints are really hurtin'. Some days it's worse than others. Today's one of 'em.'

Gideon inspected his extended hands, feeling the thick, slightly bent fingers and enlarged knuckles.

'How long have you been like this?'

'Four or five weeks. It comes and goes, but lately it's come and never left.'

He bent the man's wrist. 'Does this hurt?'

'Yeah. My right knee hurts worse, though.'

'How do you feel otherwise?'

'Kinda tired—almost like I got a flu-bug that I can't get rid of. My legs seem weak and shaky, too.'

'Have you noticed any rashes on your body? Done any traveling? How about headaches or a stiff neck?'

Carpenter screwed up his face. 'No travelin' and no rashes that I can remember.' He rubbed his forehead. 'Now that you mention it, I have had more headaches. My neck's sort of stiff and sore, too.'

'When was your last physical?'

Carpenter looked sheepish. 'Don't rightly recall,

Doc. I wouldn't be here now if my brother hadn't nagged me into coming. Nothin' you can do for arthritis, anyway.'

'Since you are here, let's give you your money's worth.' While Gideon carried out a more complete examination he continued, 'What do you do for a living, Mr Carpenter?'

The patient's grin spread from ear to ear. 'With a name like mine, I couldn't take up any other trade.'

Gideon smiled. 'I suppose not. What kind of carpentry work do you specialize in?'

'My brother Charlie and I build houses. The best in the county,' the older man boasted. 'I work on the outside and he does the finish work inside. Don't have the patience he does when it comes to detail work.'

Gideon motioned for him to lie down while he continued.

'Charlie and me are bachelors. We spend our free time makin' stuff to sell at craft shows; I cut the wood and Charlie fancies them up. Do pretty good, too.'

'I'm looking for a small display case to hold a thimble collection,' Gideon remarked, percussing the man's chest. 'Can you make something like that?'

'No problem. In fact, Charlie finished one the other night. Tell you what, Doc. I'll bring it by and you can see if it's somethin' you'd like.'

'Great. My sister's birthday is at the end of next month and I'd like to surprise her.' Gideon helped Carpenter to a sitting position, the paper sheet crackling with every move. While Mr Carpenter buttoned his shirt Gideon leaned against the counter and scribbled on the chart.

'So what's wrong with me?'

A few seconds elapsed as Gideon finished his note

and closed the manila file. Looking directly at his patient, he said, 'Your joints *are* swollen. You may have arthritis.'

The carpenter's shoulders slumped, and his gaze dropped to stare at the gnarled fingers resting in his lap. Gideon understood his worry—to a man whose livelihood depended on his hands an incapacitating disease would be devastating.

He hastened to add, 'There are different forms of arthritis, and not all of them are crippling.'

Mr Carpenter raised his head, hope flaring in his eyes.

'I'm not totally convinced that it's your problem. Your stiff neck, flu-like symptoms and headaches point to a few other diseases as well. So, I want you in the hospital for tests.'

'Geez, Doc.' Carpenter shook his head. 'I don't have time. 'Sides, I'm not that sick.'

Gideon dropped his arms and crossed them at the wrists while one hand still gripped the folder. 'I want to do a spinal tap and some blood tests, to try and pinpoint your problem. If everything checks out, I'll send you home in a couple of days.'

'Sure thing.' Carpenter's unhappiness was evident.

'I'll call the hospital right now, so go straight to the admitting office. As soon as you're settled I'll do the lumbar puncture, to remove some of the fluid in your spinal column.' Gideon quickly explained the procedure.

'As with any medical test, there are risks associated with it. In your case, the benefits of discovering a disease outweigh any potential side effects.'

Leaving his patient, Gideon spied Becky in the hallway. Handing her the chart, he apprised her of the situation. 'I want a CBC, sed rate, routine blood chem-istries, a rheumatoid factor test, and an ANA for auto-immune disorders. Don't forget the LE cell prep for lupus, and the test for Lyme Disease.'

The morning passed quickly as he dealt with an assortment of ailments. Before he realized it, Becky was announcing his last patient.

'I can't get rid of this, Dr Alexander,' thirty-five-year-old Edith Rawlings announced, holding out her arm for his inspection. 'It's getting worse, too.'

Gideon noted a line of three round, weeping lesions traveling up her wrist and forearm. Tugging on pair of disposable gloves, he hooked one foot around the stool to wheel it closer to Edith's chair. 'What happened?' he asked as he sat next to her.

'About a month ago I was cutting a few roses for my table and scratched my index finger on a thorn. I didn't think anything about it—after all, a person can't run to the doctor for every scratch.

'Anyway, I washed my hands and disinfected it right away. A few days later, I noticed a hard lump under the skin, but I figured it wasn't anything.'

She took a deep breath. 'Then the lump broke open and my skin turned black. I thought I'd developed some infection, so I bought some of that over-the-counter antibiotic cream to use. I used nearly a whole tube, but it didn't help. Now it's spreading.' She pointed to the dark lesions.

'You've picked up a fungal infection, which is why your antibiotic cream didn't work. Those ointments only work against bacteria. I suspect you have what's known as sporotrichosis; it infects the lymphatic system, which is why it's moving up your arm.'

'Oh, my gosh,' she gasped, her eyes wide. 'It sounds

terrible. Is it deadly?' Her mouth trembled. 'Will you have to. . .to. . .amputate?'

Gideon hid a smile. 'Oh, no, it's very treatable. It's a common fungus, often associated with roses, hay and wood. Horticulturists and farmers frequently become infected. It won't disappear as quickly as a bacterial infection, though.'

Edith sighed with relief and looked less panic-stricken. 'And the black spots?'

'Those are areas of dead skin cells. They'll slough off and be replaced. I'll give you a prescription, but first I want to culture one of the lesions. If the lab finds something different, I may need to change your medicine. Either way, I'll call you when I receive a report.'

'Sounds fine.'

He yanked out a drawer, expecting to grab the culture swabs and finding none. Hoping they'd arrived, and that Becky had stored them in the supply closet, he checked there first.

They were noticeably absent.

Irritated that no one had gone after them this morning, and frustrated with himself for forgetting them yesterday, he spoke to the shadow falling over his view.

'When will I get those sterile transport swabs? I need them *now*.'

Gideon pivoted to face his familiar nurse, but his mouth dropped at the sight of Natalie balancing a bulky box in her arms.

She thrust it against his chest so hard that he staggered backwards. Exaggerating a smile, she asked, 'Is this fast enough for you?'

# CHAPTER THREE

GIDEON's forehead unfurrowed and his widened eyes returned to a normal size. 'Thanks,' he said, grabbing two swabs before handing the cardboard container to Becky, who had just come upon the scene.

'Don't leave,' he ordered over his shoulder as he walked toward room two, the door swinging behind him.

'Is he always this bossy?' Natalie asked his nurse when they were alone.

Becky shrugged. 'I've only been around him for a few days, but it comes with the territory, doesn't it?'

Natalie smiled. 'Domineering 101' was obviously a required class in all medical students' curricula. 'How long will he be?'

'He's with his last patient right now. His office is at the end of the hall if you'd like to wait there.'

While Becky resumed her nursing duties Natalie meandered toward Gideon's office. After Becky had called, begging for someone to bring the supplies as soon as possible, she'd volunteered out of curiosity rather than courtesy; she wanted to see how 'her' money had been spent.

Two landscapes caught her eye, and she paused to study them. Like those in his waiting-room, the art-work depicted recognizable Colorado mountain scenes. While the others captured the flavor of autumn and winter, these two froze moments of spring and summer splendor. The artist's shades blended with the light

41

gray hues of the walls, and she wondered if Gideon's color scheme had been by design or coincidence.

Jealousy reared its green head and she forced it away. It was too late for regrets and recriminations; she needed to be thankful that her equipment order hadn't been canceled.

The door to his office stood open and Natalie stepped inside. Although she detected a slight medicinal odor, she also caught a lingering aroma of his woodsy aftershave.

At the same time she noticed a picture of an eagle, soaring above snow-capped mountains. On closer inspection she saw it had been a thousand-piece puzzle at one time, now shellacked and framed as a testimony to the hours spent in its creation.

Eager to learn more, she glanced around the room. It fit her perception of a typical physician's office, with its standard bookcase lined with medical tomes and magazines, a utilitarian desk and chair, and a framed medical school diploma.

The marks and occasional gouges on the sturdy furniture suggested that he'd either used the pieces for a long time or had bought them secondhand. The desktop was uncluttered, although a few medical journals and papers lay haphazardly on the surface.

A snapshot of him surrounded by people with a marked resemblance—obviously his family—leaned against an engraved pen holder. An opened magazine lay next to it—a crossword puzzle magazine.

She grinned. She hadn't worked on one for ages. Pulling the publication closer, she saw one page half completed. Unable to resist, she tested her skill.

Twelve across, eight letters. Repentant. 'Penitent,'

she supplied out loud. Amused by her success, she continued.

Major artery. Beginning with the letter A. 'Aorta,' she murmured, not surprised that he'd filled in those blanks.

Unable to hear. Seeing the four squares empty, she wrote the word 'deaf'.

Delivers babies. She thought a moment. Obstetrician? No, that wasn't right; it was a five-letter word. That also eliminated doctor and midwife.

While concentrating on other possibilities her gaze fell again on the photo, on Gideon in particular. She wondered what he had been like as a youngster. Had he been as serious as now, or had life's circumstances cut short his boyhood?

Would his children be the same? Or would they resemble their mother? She grinned, thinking of toddlers with his features stamped across their faces. What would it be like to have his child. . .to have his hands caress her skin, his unique male scent filling her nostrils, his full lips pressed against hers. . . ?

Natalie caught her breath once she realized her daydream had ventured into exciting yet inaccessible territory. Her handicap had turned off several men she'd been interested in, and those it hadn't had overlooked her imperfection only in order to gain her father's favor. She wasn't about to learn which of those two categories applied to Gideon—or any other male, for that matter. A person could only stand so much rejection, and she'd reached her limit.

Pushing aside her painful memories, she reread the clue. 'Who delivers babies? A five-letter word with an "o" in the middle,' she mused aloud, focusing on her tapping pencil rather than on her intimate picture of the well-built physician.

'Think what, not who,' suggested a male voice from the doorway.

She jumped. The sight of Gideon in the flesh sent heat pulsing through her body, especially when her gaze lingered on his lips. 'What? Oh, what.' Composing herself, she shook her head. 'I don't know the names of the instruments, other than forceps, and that doesn't fit either.' His deep laugh made her bewilderment grow.

'My, my. All that medical training and she doesn't know the stork delivers babies,' Gideon chortled.

His humor was contagious and she grinned. 'The education system today isn't what it used to be. Now you know why crossword puzzles aren't my hobby.'

'What *does* Natalie Canfield do in her spare time?' he asked, leaning against the doorjamb.

'It's in very short supply,' she admitted, 'but I work on counted cross-stitch projects when I'm not coaching the Rocky Hills' Swimmers.'

'No kidding? My sister Katie was on Leadville's high school team. She's sixteen, by the way. We assumed that she wouldn't have an opportunity to continue.'

'No one mentioned the youth activities?' Surprised by the oversight, Natalie distinctly remembered how Bill Burns had promoted the community during her own interviews. Once again, she wondered why Gideon had moved to a town he knew so little about.

'I never asked. Then again, I didn't concern myself with schools at the time I was. . .er. . .negotiating my contract. Katie didn't decide to move in with me until a few weeks ago.'

'Oh.' She'd forgotten about Mrs Alexander's death.

Gideon moved away from the door. 'She's interested in a medical career, and thought she'd get a better idea of its demands if she lived with her doctor brother.'

'Sounds like a smart decision.'

'In theory, yes. I don't know how good I'll be with the so-called "girl" things, though. It's nice coming home to someone, but I worry that she doesn't have a woman's influence. She might be better off with my brother and his family.'

Natalie shrugged. 'It's important for her to be in a comfortable environment. Maybe she'd rather have your sole attention—more or less—instead of being one in a crowd.'

Gideon rubbed his jaw, his mood thoughtful. 'I hadn't considered that,' he finally conceded.

'If she's interested in swimming, we have regular practice on Tuesday and Thursday evenings, as well as Saturday mornings. I'm having a make-up session tonight for those who've missed the last few times. Katie's welcome to join us, or she can wait until tomorrow morning. We begin at eight a.m. Sharp.'

'Do you have tryouts?'

Natalie shook her head. 'We want as many kids to participate as possible. Although they do compete against each other, we stress improvement, not winning. Paying the fees is our only requirement.'

'Of course. By the way, thanks for delivering those lab supplies.'

'No problem. I'm curious, though. Why did you open your office on a Friday? I'm surprised you didn't wait until Monday.'

'Several reasons. One, I thought it would be better to begin with a light schedule and iron out any problems like the culture supplies before I have a full waiting-room. Secondly, I agreed to begin August fifteenth. I didn't pay attention to the day of the week it fell on.'

Impressed by his commitment, her gaze moved to his diploma. Although she hadn't planned to mention her father, her question popped out of her mouth. 'Did you know a Dr Harrison Pike while you were in med school?'

'Why do you ask?'

She shrugged, wishing her tongue hadn't disconnected from her brain. 'We've referred some of our orthopedic patients to him. I've heard he's excellent.'

'Oh, he is,' he affirmed.

'Then you know him?' she persisted.

'Yes, I do.'

Her body tensed and her breath froze in her chest.

'You can't attend *any* medical school without knowing or hearing about Harrison Pike,' Gideon clarified. 'I met him after one of his lectures. He's an incredible speaker, but internists don't deal very often with orthopedic surgeons, no matter how famous.'

Natalie relaxed, satisfied by his responses. His comments, combined with his brusque manner toward her at times, had put her fears of a connection between him and her dad to rest.

Glancing at her watch, she rose. She'd never expected to enjoy the spur of the moment visit, but she had. 'Sorry to run, but my lunchbreak is over. Did you want something?'

Gideon's tone became businesslike. 'Can you handle fungal cultures in your lab, or do you send them to another facility? Mrs Rawlings presents a classic picture of sporotrichosis, but I want it confirmed.'

'Yes, but that species of fungus doesn't show up very

well on direct microscopic exam. You may have to wait until something grows on the agar,' she warned. 'And fungi require several weeks.'

'No problem. Have you found anything on Coffman yet?'

His emphasis on 'yet' came through loud and clear. 'I called in my preliminary report early this morning,' she said stiffly. 'Bacteria is present, and appears to be a strain of staph or strep.' The words 'you were right' hung in the air as if they'd been spoken.

'Any ideas which one?' Gideon's smug smile grated on her nerves.

'I can't say for certain until I have a colony to work with,' she prevaricated, although she had her own ideas.

When she'd first seen the cloudy blood culture bottle, which should have been clear, she'd hoped to find an agent he hadn't expected.

'Come now,' he coaxed. 'I know you can give me a presumptive identification. Microbiologists do it all the time. At least they do in Denver.'

His implication that she couldn't make an elementary judgement call didn't escape her notice. 'It resembles a staphylococcus,' she ground out, folding her arms. 'The gram-positive cocci appear in clusters, rather than the typical chains that strep forms. Satisfied?'

'Definitely.'

She'd wanted—no, ached—to prove him wrong. Unfortunately she hadn't, and from the glimmer of his pearly white teeth she suspected that he knew it, too. Darn. Why did this arrogant man have such an endearing dimple?

'Anything else?' she asked, keeping her voice cool.

'As a matter of fact, there is one more thing,' he said. 'What do you know about Lyme Disease?'

From the look on his face, he expected her to answer 'not much'. She squared her shoulders and recited all the facts she remembered. 'It was first identified in the town of Lyme, Connecticut, after a large number of juvenile arthritis cases were reported in 1976. Europeans have other names for it, although I'm not certain what they are—Erythema Migrans comes to mind.'

She drew a breath and continued. 'It's caused by a spirochete—a spiral-shaped bacteria—which is carried by a tick. There's a characteristic rash associated with the bite, but not always present. There's also—'

Gideon held up his hands in a classic 'stop' position. 'I get the picture. You're obviously familiar with this condition.'

'Some of us read our professional journals, even if we don't work in Denver.'

He saluted. 'Touché, Ms Canfield. Have you had any cases in the area?'

'No. We've sent a number of samples for testing, but none has been positive.'

He briefly outlined John Carpenter's symptoms. 'I'm on my way to perform his spinal tap, and I'll want the fluid checked for Lyme Disease in addition to the routine tests.'

Her concern for the patient softened her animosity. 'We'll have a report from our reference lab in a few days,' she promised.

'Is that the best you can do?'

Inwardly she bristled at his disbelieving tone. 'I'm afraid so, Doctor. When you're on the last outpost of civilization, you have to make some allowances.'

Turning on her heel, she grabbed several specimen bags from Becky and bid her a curt goodbye before striding across the rain-spattered parking lot and into her cramped quarters. She plunked her cargo into the nearly full 'In' basket before slipping on her lab coat.

'Enjoy your lunch?' Karen asked.

'Yes and no.'

'Did you tangle with Dr Alexander?' Karen sounded like a mother about to chastise her child.

'Not really,' Natalie admitted. 'He makes me feel. . .' She paused, searching for the right descriptive word. 'Frustrated, I guess.'

'I told you to go out with Jason Wyman when he asked you the other night. Then you wouldn't have thoughts like that, if you know what I mean.' She wiggled her eyebrows over her reading-glasses.

Natalie buttoned her lab coat. 'Well, I wasn't referring to a sexual kind of frustration. Mine is the can't-get-anywhere-because-I'm-swimming-upstream-type. It just kills me to tell Dr Alexander that we can't do things as efficiently as he's used to. He must think we're incompetent.'

'Don't be so hard on yourself. Small facilities like ours can't provide the same service a large referral center does. It has nothing to do with our personal skills.'

Natalie paused. 'You're right. This is a touchy subject for me. When I know what we're capable of doing, it isn't easy to send those tests to another laboratory.'

'Cheer up. Our accountant and purchasing officer asked to meet with you at four o'clock. I'm sure you'll hear good news—like when our automated organism identification instrument will arrive.'

'We can always hope,' Natalie replied, her spirits

lifting. She couldn't wait to prove to her father that she could succeed without his intervention or coddling.

Turning her attention to the incoming specimens, she thumbed through several requisitions. 'Stool cultures? *Ten* of them?'

Karen nodded. 'Unusual, isn't it? I haven't had a chance to check out the situation, but there must be a very nasty bug going around.'

'I'd better phone in our supply order,' Natalie mused. 'I'd hate to run short.'

The afternoon flew by, with both women working steadily. While Karen prepared the drug sensitivity tests before she left for the day Natalie took to the microscope.

'Uh-oh,' Natalie remarked after focusing on the image. 'Looks like Happy Hearts Preschool needs to change their name to Happy Hands. I found a pinworm.'

After checking another sample, she commented, 'Make that two out of two.'

'I hope they treat the whole bunch this time, and not just a few,' Karen remarked.

'I agree. Gosh, can you imagine dealing with twenty-some infected toddlers?'

'No, but I bet there will be at least that many mothers washing towels and bedding tonight.'

Karen stacked her Petri plates in the incubator and closed the door. 'That's it for today, boss. The place is all yours. Try not to find anything else to do.'

Natalie grinned. 'I'll do my best.'

Working alone, she scanned Edith Rawlings' direct smear of her skin lesions. Although finding the fungus in its characteristic yeast phase of growth was a longshot, she kept a watchful eye out for any cigar-shaped structures.

Minutes ticked by. She'd decided to declare 'no fungal elements observed', when one caught her attention. Several fields later, she located a few more forms.

He's right again, she thought with grudging admiration. Gideon Alexander, at this point in time, could be considered a valuable addition to St Mark's medical staff.

She had been too critical of the doctor, she decided as she examined John Carpenter's spinal fluid and found no bacteria present. At least the department's funds were benefiting a doctor with expertise, not someone mediocre or haphazard. So what if he'd caused her a few setbacks? She'd meet her goals as long as she concentrated on the future instead of the past.

Bolstered by the thought, she tidied the countertops and went to her meeting.

'I'm afraid you won't like my news,' Ben Watson, the accountant, told her. 'I had to void several equipment purchase orders.'

Natalie's cheerfulness drained away like rinse water. She shook her head and clasped her hands together. 'If one of those was mine, you'd better rethink your decision,' she warned him, fighting for calm.

'I can't.' The thirty-year-old prematurely bald accountant looked apologetic.

'Correct me if I'm wrong, but didn't you say when you canceled my remodeling project, "Don't worry, Natalie. You won't lose anything else?"' she reminded him. 'I need my instrument.'

'I know. Unfortunately it can't be helped.'

'Why not?' she crossed her arms.

'Finances are tight. Expenses are up, revenue is down, and we're cutting costs wherever we can.'

She scoffed. 'You've been saying that ever since I came. Why is there always money for other pet projects? I'm sure the hospital's party for Dr Alexander didn't come cheap.'

'Those items were budgeted.'

'So was mine.'

'I know, and I'm sorry. You'll get it next time.'

'I want it in writing. Preferably in blood.'

Ben guffawed, and the silent purchasing officer joined in. 'Good joke. You thought we wouldn't catch it, didn't you—working in the lab and wanting it written in blood?'

She faked a smile, then wiped it away. 'What will the money be used for?'

The two men looked at each other. 'We aren't applying it to anything specific. Several other expenditures ran higher than we'd anticipated, and we have to juggle the numbers a little bit.'

'Hmm. Robbing my department to pay. . .for Dr Alexander's offices, perhaps?' she asked, staring first at one man then the other.

Ben squirmed in his padded chair.

'I see,' she said, aware that her voice quivered.

'Without doctors we won't need a lab—microbiology or otherwise,' Ben reminded her.

Natalie rose, her head high. 'And without a lab they can't serve their patients.' With her throat burning and her chest aching, she stormed back to her territory.

She'd chosen St Mark's instead of another facility because the management team had claimed to share her vision of providing previously unavailable services to the community.

They needed a state-of-the-art microbiology lab, she'd been told, to attract physicians to the area. Thrilled to have an opportunity to improve this area of the hospital, she'd accepted the position without any second thoughts. Now, two years later, she questioned her decision. After all of her hard work, her extensive justifications and proposals, she still had little to show for her efforts.

She yearned for the day when she'd prove her competence without her family's intervention. They had each made a name for themselves in their field—her father in orthopedics, her brother as an attorney, her sister as an educator. She wanted to do the same.

Sadly that day had slipped out of reach. Again.

Frustration climbed to mountain heights, and she decided to vent it before she lost her composure in public. Grabbing her purse, she left the building, jumped into her Volkswagen and headed for the high school swimming pool.

Once there, Natalie found the smell of chlorine comforting in its familiarity. She slipped into the locker-room to change into the swimwear she carried with her on practice days, grateful for an hour to herself before the students arrived.

The water in the Olympic-sized pool looked like clear plate glass, and she couldn't wait to jump into its tranquil depths. Standing near the edge, she replaced her small hearing aids with molded earplugs and stored them in her bag.

Assuming the startoff position, she dove into the heated water, cutting it with surgical precision and a steady rhythm.

Silence surrounded her. Total, absolute silence. At times it was welcome, and this was one of them.

Swimming freestyle, she quickly covered the twenty-five meters, flipped, then repeated the lap. Back and forth she went, pushing everything out of her mind to concentrate on her form.

By the time she grew tired she'd covered several kilometers with every stroke imaginable. Hanging onto the edge of the pool, she panted, trying to catch her breath.

Thank goodness Ben had sprung his news on her today—Friday. With any luck, she'd have all weekend to come to terms with her latest setback before encountering the man responsible.

'Hurry up, Gideon,' Katie scolded as she stood at the door with her duffle bag slung over one shoulder. 'I don't want to be late.'

Gideon washed down his last bite of cherry pie with decaffeinated coffee. 'I'm not letting my favourite dessert go to waste,' he said, rising to rinse his plate.

'Leave it,' she ordered, fidgeting in the doorway. 'I'll wash up later. Come on.'

'Sorry, Kate. Old habits are hard to break. If it will make you happy, though, I'll make a point to save all my dirty dishes for you,' he joked.

'Oh, you know what I mean,' she replied, sounding exasperated as she tapped one foot.

'Are you sure you want to walk? It looks like it could rain again.'

'It's only cloudy,' she replied, shoving him through the door. 'For your information, I timed myself the other day, and it takes five minutes to walk to school.'

'Regular walking or power walking?' he asked. falling into step beside her.

'Regular. So if we hurry, we'll make it in two or three.'

Gideon smiled at Katie's excitement. When he had casually asked if she wanted to join a swim team, she had squealed and run over to hug him until his ribs had ached. He hadn't realized until then that her nonchalance over her lost swimming opportunities had been faked.

'I don't understand why you wanted to come along,' Katie said now. 'I'm not six years old.'

'I know.' Looking down on her brown hair, so much like his own, he smiled. 'Since I'm free this evening, I wanted to watch. Besides, I need to see if you're as good as you claim.'

She punched him on the arm. 'Of course I am. And I have the medals and trophies to prove it.' Speeding up the last path, she left him a few steps behind.

Although he truly did want to watch his sister go through her paces, he had another reason for coming. He wanted to see Natalie. Only because he had a mission, he told himself, ignoring his rush of anticipation. Personal relationships had to be based on honesty—something already lacking between them.

As he entered the natatorium, a warm blast of chlorine-laden air hit him, making it difficult to breathe for a minute. At the same time he saw the L-shaped body of water sparkling under the incandescent lights.

The last pool he'd visited had been at the YMCA, and it didn't compare at all to this one. Instead of dingy gray, the walls were bright blue with black distance markings. Multi-colored flags stretched across the watery expanse in the well-lit room and a floating walkway separated the short leg of the L from the lap lanes.

'Neat pool,' Katie breathed.

He nodded, accepting her decision as expert although he concurred.

The warm, moist air soon made his skin clammy. He wiped away a few sweat beads from his forehead, grateful for Katie's suggestion that he change into a polo shirt and shorts. Wearing dress clothes for two hours in this humidity would have been pure torture.

Glancing around, he saw Natalie at the opposite end of the pool, inspecting the mounting blocks. Pointing to her, he said, 'There's your coach.'

His voice, although not purposely loud, echoed in the huge expanse. Surprised by Natalie's lack of response, he approached her with his sister in tow. As he came closer he noticed that a huge T-shirt covered her swimsuit and that her hair hung in wet ringlets.

'Hi, Natalie,' he said to her back.

She didn't face him. Puzzled by the situation, he glanced at Katie before stepping closer.

Suddenly Natalie turned and drew in a sharp, startled breath. Thinking shock accounted for her dismayed expression, he opened his mouth to speak. But before he could utter a syllable, she directed a smile to the girl at his side. 'You must be Katie.'

Katie nodded.

Strangely enough, Gideon felt left out, even though he knew that her newest charge demanded her whole attention.

'I understand you have competitive swimming experience,' Natalie said.

'I placed first in the freestyle and backstroke events for our district,' Katie announced with pride.

'How are your butterfly and breast strokes?'

'Not as good,' the girl admitted. 'I was working on them when. . .before I left Leadville.'

'She's still better than most,' Gideon interjected.

Natalie continued as if he hadn't spoken. 'We're glad to have you join us.'

Gideon's annoyance began to build. Why was Natalie ignoring him? Didn't she know the rudiments of creating a rapport with parents and carers?

Pointing to her right, Natalie said, 'The locker-room is through that door. After you've changed, warm up with a few laps. Then you can show me your stuff.'

The moment Natalie's head turned away, Gideon saw the earplugs through her tangled hair. Earplugs molded to fit so perfectly that they had to have been custom-made.

Other observations clicked together—the way she hadn't heard the echo or their approach, the way her gaze had lingered on Katie's mouth.

His heart sank. He had totally misjudged the situation. Now he understood why Harrison Pike wanted 'insurance' for his daughter; why he was so protective—to the point of calling in special favors on her behalf.

Natalie was deaf.

# CHAPTER FOUR

FROZEN to the spot, Gideon watched Natalie through analytical eyes. How had he missed her handicap? He was a physician, for heaven's sakes. Of all people, *he* should have noticed her impairment.

In retrospect, he couldn't recall any mannerisms providing distinct clues. Even when he'd approached her unawares in his office he hadn't done anything unusual to attract her attention. And yet, from the way she had interacted with Katie, Natalie read lips with far more expertise than someone with minimal hearing loss. Her case must be severe, he decided, although she obviously had enough auditory capability for a mechanical device to be effective.

As soon as Katie had headed for the women's locker-room, Natalie turned away. Without thinking of the reasons why he wanted a few minutes of her time, Gideon clasped her shoulder. Through the damp coverup the hard ridge of her suit's spaghetti strap pressed into his palm. At the same time he became acutely aware of a dainty bone-structure, in spite of her height.

Natalie stared at him, her eyes glittering pools of disappointment, discouragement and wariness.

Surprised by her emotions, he asked, 'Is something wrong?' She'd been so animated when she talked to Katie only a few seconds ago.

Natalie shrugged, her mouth drawn into a line. 'Busy day.'

'Problems?'

'Yeah. You could say that.'

He paused, waiting for her to elaborate.

'Did you want something, Dr Alexander?' she countered, raising one brown eyebrow.

His hand dropped. 'Can we dispense with formality? At least when we're off duty?'

Natalie tugged a lock of wet hair over one ear. 'I suppose so,' she finally said.

'Good.' He grinned, hoping to set her at ease.

'Did you need something?' She rephrased her question, her tone cool and her expression indifferent.

His smile died as swiftly as his attempts to make conversation. He fingered the house keys in his shorts pocket and followed her lead. 'Are there forms to fill out? Permission slips, medical authorizations—that kind of thing?'

She nodded. 'There are a few. I'll give them to Katie before she leaves.'

The sound of voices intruded. Gideon glanced over his shoulder to find a trio of two boys and a girl, all appearing close to Katie's age, walking toward them.

'Hi, coach,' the tallest youth called out as he signed his greeting.

'Hi, Adam. I'm glad to see you three could make it,' Natalie replied aloud, her hands gracefully conveying the same message.

With her students now claiming her attention, Gideon climbed the stairs to the spectators' gallery and chose a seat with an unobstructed view—an easy task since he had no one else vying for a choice spot. From his vantage point, he watched Natalie insert her hearing-aids before hanging a stopwatch and whistle around her neck.

For the next two hours he sat engrossed in the proceedings, often mentally urging Katie on as Natalie timed her during various heats. If he'd had any subconscious doubts about Natalie's coaching abilities, they had disappeared within the first hour.

'Come on, Adam, keep your palms facing out.'

'Katie, don't forget to point your toes.'

'Richard, you're not kicking hard enough.'

'Sara, arch your back more as you swing your arms.'

Occasionally heads would bob to the surface, listen for a few seconds, then duck underwater. It was obvious that Natalie expected their best efforts, and the teens responded to her commands like puppies trying to please.

She used her whistle judiciously—to start a timed race or to gain someone's attention when her voice didn't carry over the churning water.

For every lap made Natalie strode along the edge of the pool, yelling instructions and shouting encouragement to the swimmers in their individual lanes. Gideon lost track of the number of meters they covered, but she walked the same distance, stopping only long enough to squeegee off the water they'd splashed onto the walkway.

While she paced he feasted on the sight of her shapely long legs, and imagined the curves hidden underneath the oversized shirt that skimmed the tops of her thighs. Each spray that caught her turned the dry fabric more transparent, and he wished to see more than a dark outline of her bathing suit. Even so, her figure was well-proportioned though not well-endowed.

The female body presented no mysteries to him *per se*, but the one before him didn't evoke his clinical interest. Too bad his hormones had decided to assert themselves over a woman where chances of gratification were nil.

He fidgeted in the hard stadium chair and rubbed the back of his neck. The sparkling water beckoned, and he wanted to dive in and cool off his overheated body. Maybe if he pictured Natalie bundled in a parka on a frigid, snowy mountaintop instead of clad in next to nothing on a sandy beach with a tropical breeze gently caressing her skin. . .

'That's it for today,' Natalie announced to her charges as they hung poolside, panting for breath. 'You did very well, guys. And girls.'

Adam hoisted himself out of the water, groaning. 'Gosh, coach. Did you have to work us so hard on our first day back? I'm pooped.'

Natalie's laugh drifted like music across the room. 'Would you like me to cancel your date for this evening so you can rest?' She struck a thoughtful pose. 'Let's see. Who is it tonight? Erica or Susan?'

Adam grinned. 'My strength's coming back.'

She smiled. 'I thought it would. Don't forget—tomorrow morning, eight o'clock sharp.'

While the four teens exited to the showers Gideon stood and stretched. Natalie, for whatever reason, hadn't wanted to talk before, but he was determined to make another effort. Even if their relationship couldn't progress to intimate levels, they had to become friends. It was the only way they'd both get what they wanted.

Natalie stuffed her wet towels into a tote bag, willing her students to hurry. Exhaustion—both mental and physical—had descended swiftly, and she wanted to lock the building, hop in her compact car and head for home.

Tension had contributed to her fatigue, too; tension generated by Gideon's presence. Parents were always welcome, but she had a hard time thinking of him as a parent or guardian. People watching their children's progress didn't pay attention to her, but Gideon did. In fact, he seemed more interested in her than in his sister.

How ironic. She'd never felt exposed in her bathing suit before, even during puberty, but today she did. Logically she knew that she looked decent, yet she felt as if she wore a shapeless hospital gown with only one fragile string in place to guard her modesty.

He'd also discovered her flaw. She'd never hidden her deafness from anyone, but she'd never flaunted it either. For the most part she considered it no worse than needing a pair of glasses to correct a vision problem. Yet, to a man as perfect as Gideon Alexander, it would be an obvious defect. She was being illogical and unreasonable, but it seemed as if he'd literally uncovered all of her secrets.

If only he he'd carried an extra thirty pounds, and sported a potbelly, receding hairline and crooked, tobacco-stained teeth. . . But he didn't.

His over-six-feet-tall frame had a solid yet trim physique, and his polo shirt—unbuttoned far enough to show the skin below the hollow of his throat— enhanced broad shoulders. A fine sprinkling of dark hair covered his muscular legs and forearms, fueling her imagination as she visualized his bared chest.

This was ridiculous, she scolded. Maybe she *should* have gone out with Jason Wyman. . .

'Do you always work them this hard?' Gideon asked from behind her.

Natalie swung around to face him. His noncommittal expression made it hard to tell if he supported or opposed her training methods.

She squared her shoulders and looked him in the eye. 'Yes.'

He nodded, as if satisfied. 'No pain, no gain.'

'Exactly.' She dug in her bag again and rummaged for Katie's promised paperwork.

'I'm surprised you made Katie work like the others. She hasn't been near a pool for several months.'

Natalie froze for a second, her suppressed anger ballooning like an aneurysm. She took a deep breath and counted to ten, drawing on reserves of willpower to keep from exploding.

'I couldn't believe—'

'Are you a swimming instructor?' she interrupted, with all the calm she could muster.

'No, but—'

'Then perhaps you might leave the coaching to me.'

'Yes, but—'

'Not only have I been involved with this program for two years, but I also began competitive swimming when I was nine. I *know* what kids can and can't do.'

'I just thought—'

'You wouldn't appreciate anyone's interference in your profession, so don't make any in mine.'

The words hovered in the humid air, swirling around and lingering like dense fog. Realizing she'd voiced her deepest thoughts, she gasped at her own audacity.

Her skin temperature rose, and she knew her face would appear as red as if it had been painted with

Mercurochrome antiseptic. Gideon might not realize the double meaning, but she certainly did.

'I'm sorry. I shouldn't have been so rude.' She apologized to his running-shoes.

Time passed slowly until he spoke. 'I was trying to say that in spite of Katie being out of practice, I couldn't believe her stamina. She kept up very well.'

His quiet tone and lack of censure worsened her guilt over acting like a troublesome toddler.

Gideon continued. 'Although I didn't know about your hearing impairment until today, in general I consider myself fairly observant. You haven't come across as someone who's normally bad-tempered, so you must have something on your mind.' He paused. 'Am I right?'

Natalie opened her mouth to deny it, but couldn't. She tugged on a lock of hair and debated her course of action. She could gloss over her lack of self-control by pleading temporary insanity brought on by a stressful day. He was a physician; he'd know what she meant.

On the other hand, she'd always hated it when her family had evaded issues under the guise of 'protecting' her, and she'd vowed never to do the same. A fine line often separated situations requiring tact versus blunt honesty, and she wondered which option fit her present predicament the best.

'Yes. Yes, you are.' She met his gaze head-on.

'Want to talk about it?'

'Not particularly.'

Gideon shifted his weight and stroked his chin. 'I see.' He paused. 'How do you suggest we work around this? We can't ignore each other.'

Natalie sighed. 'I know.'

'Are you sure you don't want to tell me what's going on?'

'No.'

Gideon raised his eyes as if seeking divine guidance. 'No, you're not sure, or no, you don't want to talk about it?'

Natalie zipped the bag. The harsh grating noise of metal teeth jarred the peaceful sound of water lapping against the cement.

'No, I don't want to discuss it, but I will.' She shrugged. 'It's rather—'

'Childish?' he supplied.

'Difficult,' she corrected, glaring at him.

Gideon leaned against the wall and looked far too relaxed and smug to suit her. But then why shouldn't he? He was right, and he knew it.

Natalie slung her bag over one shoulder. 'My funding was cut. Again, I might add. I found out late this afternoon.'

He lost his teasing expression. 'I'm sorry.' His brow furrowed, as if he'd drawn an unpleasant conclusion. 'And you think I'm responsible.'

'Indirectly, you are.'

'How so?'

'Hospital expenditures supposedly ran over budget. A new doctor's office comes to mind.'

He rubbed his chin. 'I don't know what to say.'

'There's nothing *to* say.'

'I *am* sorry.' His eyes showed pain.

Natalie shrugged.

'You said "again". What did you mean?'

'Just forget it,' she replied, waving her hand in the air as if she could erase the subject by doing so. 'It doesn't matter. It's in the past and can't be changed.'

She turned toward the exit, willing herself to follow her own good advice.

He grabbed her elbow and held it in a firm grip. 'It *does* matter,' he insisted, fixing her to the spot and stepping into her line of vision.

Gideon was determined to get his answers; the rigid set of his mouth and the firm line of his jaw said so. Hoping to end this conversation before the teenagers reappeared, she took a deep breath and began.

'My department's remodeling project was scheduled for this fall. It was canceled. Last April.'

The timing of events must have hit home, because he released her arm as if he'd touched hot coals.

'What makes the situation hard to swallow is that when you leave—and you will—we'll suffer through the same financial juggling in order to attract the next physician.'

She'd expected a snappy comeback, or at least something similar to the accountant's comment, not utter silence and a bleak expression. At the very minimum she wanted him to contradict her and insist that he was at St Mark's to stay.

The seconds ticked by. Each one reaffirmed her guess—his commitment to the community would end the moment his contract expired.

His dismay was obvious, and she felt badly for being so blunt. For the last several hours she'd imagined telling Gideon the unvarnished truth, receiving a great deal of satisfaction from her fantasy. Unfortunately, unburdening her soul had simply made them both miserable. She should have kept her own counsel and let time heal her latest resentment.

She placed a hand on his forearm. 'Look. I'm sorry for implying that you were responsible, when it was a situation totally out of your control. It would have happened with any doctor Bill Burns recruited.'

Teenage voices and high-pitched giggles heralded the four swimmers' approach. Natalie closed her eyes and offered a mental 'thank you' for the interruption. 'Ready, guys?' she asked, digging the school keys out of her bag's side pocket.

Without waiting for a reply, she led the small group toward the exit and locked the double doors behind them. The cool breeze and pleasant early evening temperatures brought on by the overcast sky created a sharp contrast to the warm humidity inside the building. The abrupt change raised goosebumps on every inch of her exposed skin and she rubbed her arms.

'Miss Canfield—er—Natalie?' Katie asked, after her teammates had said their goodbyes and cut across the soggy lawn in three different directions.

Natalie tucked the keyring into her bag. 'Yes?'

'I wondered if, the next time you have a special practice—' Katie glanced at her brother, as if gaining his approval '—you'd call me?'

'Of course. I thought you did very well this evening.'

The girl shrugged, although her wide smile and pink face revealed her pleasure with the compliment. 'They're quite a bit better than I am.'

'After you've trained for a few weeks you'll swim circles around these guys,' Natalie replied, hugging her close.

Her heart went out to the motherless girl, and she remembered Gideon's concerns about his sister not having a woman's influence. After their heated exchange, she might not be the female role model he had in mind, but she wanted at least to try.

'If you'd like, and it's okay with big brother,

we'll stop for a hamburger sometime.'

Katie's head bobbed up and down.

Glancing at Gideon, Natalie wasn't prepared to see his frown or his furrowed eyebrows while he considered her invitation. She heard the clink of either keys or coins coming from his pocket. Fearing she might become a bone of contention between the two Alexanders, she was ready to retract her offer when Katie interrupted.

'Gideon?' she pleaded.

He jerked, then settled his gaze on his sister. 'Fine. Fine with me.' His mouth curved just enough for a faint dimple to appear in his cheek, his eyes glittering with love as he stared down at her.

Moved by the sight, Natalie blinked several times and swallowed the lump forming in her throat.

'Anytime,' he added, addressing Natalie.

His noncommittal expression didn't give a single clue to indicate how he truly felt, but the die was cast, and it was too late now for him to say no. Regardless of her schedule, she would carve out time for Katie Alexander.


'Does this hurt, Mrs Patterson?' Gideon asked the overweight woman as he pressed on her upper abdomen. He had just walked into the hospital for Sunday evening rounds when he'd been asked to take an unassigned patient.

She gasped. 'I should say so, Doctor,' she retorted, somewhat breathlessly. 'Must you keep doing that? Honestly, can't you take my word that it hurts? Oh, my, I'm going to be sick.'

She covered her mouth, turned her head, and rolled onto her side. Sally, an ER nurse, supplied an emesis basin from a bedside table without a second to spare.

While Mrs Patterson emptied her stomach the non-clinical side of Gideon's mind wandered. Katie's excitement over swimming on Rocky Hills' team hadn't dimmed one iota all weekend; she'd become the exuberant young girl he remembered from before their mother had died. He hated to admit it, but he had to—indirectly, he owed Harrison Pike for Katie's attitude-change.

If only he knew how he could convince the management team to reverse their decision regarding Natalie's request. Talking to the accountant wouldn't help; the hospital couldn't spend money it didn't have.

His personal problems faded into the background as soon as Mrs Patterson's retching stopped. She rolled onto her back and dotted her forehead with a lace-trimmed handkerchief while Sally whisked the bowl out of sight. A variety of expensive rings encircled the patient's pudgy fingers and a double strand of pink pearls hung around her neck. Her cloying scent of gardenias—so powerful that it made Gideon's eyes water—masked the usual hospital disinfectant odor.

Her make-up, even though heavily applied, didn't conceal the pallor underneath. Not one wisp of hair had fallen out of place, in spite of her head hanging over a pan several times. It didn't dare, Gideon thought.

'Elmer? Elmer, are you still here?' she demanded.

Mr Patterson rose off his chair in the corner to stand near the foot of the bed. 'Yes, Maude, I am.'

Although Maude wore a cotton hospital gown, her sparsely-haired husband was dressed in an expensive-looking navy suit.

'Be a dear and get an antacid out of my purse.'

'I have to say no,' Gideon interjected, freezing the man with his tone. 'I'll order something for the pain in a few minutes.'

'Then can we get on with it?' Mrs Patterson huffed.

'Just as soon as I get some information,' Gideon placated her. 'When did you start having problems?' He pushed one of the bed's control buttons until the head rose to a forty-five-degree angle.

'About an hour after we ate. The Montgomerys served the most *delightful* meal. They're gourmet cooks, you know. I've never had Beef Wellington like theirs. Simply fabulous.' She closed her eyes, licked her lips, and sighed.

Gideon kept his face impassive. Eating was obviously her passion, and something she wouldn't easily modify even though her health demanded it. 'Have you had these episodes before?' he asked, guessing her answer.

'Once in a while.'

'She has them quite frequently,' her husband corrected.

'How often?' Gideon stuck his stethoscope in his ears and listened to her heart and lung sounds.

Maude waved her hand, as if she considered the question immaterial, her diamonds sparkling under the fluorescent lights. 'A few times a week.'

'When was your last physical?'

'I haven't seen a doctor in years, at least not since old Dr Baker died in seventy-eight. Besides, I'm never sick.'

'You are now.' Gideon straightened, slinging the instrument around his neck.

'Will you please give me some medicine to take care of this, Doctor? We have a bridge party waiting for our return, and it's already after eight.'

'I'm afraid you'll miss this one, since you won't be leaving tonight. I want several tests run before I send you home.'

'This is preposterous. It's only a severe case of indigestion, young man. I think I know when I'm sick enough to stay in a hospital.'

Gideon crossed his arms. 'The problem is your gallbladder, not indigestion. Your history suggests it's been inflamed for some time and is obviously becoming worse. Now, you *can* leave—but if you do, it will be against my advice, and I can guarantee you'll be back.'

Maude's lips were drawn into a tight circle, her penciled-in eyebrows forming a straight line.

Gideon tried his most persuasive tone. 'Wouldn't you rather stay and let us correct your condition before it becomes an emergency?'

Holding her abdomen, Maude swung her thick legs over the edge of the bed and sat upright. 'Get my clothes, Elmer. I'm leaving.'

Mr Patterson rubbed his nearly bald pate, chewed on his lower lip and shifted his weight several times.

'What are you waiting for?' she shrilled.

Elmer glanced at Gideon, then the nurse, then back at Gideon.

Gideon crossed his arms and raised one eyebrow, waiting for a decision.

Suddenly Elmer straightened his shoulders and stretched to his full five and a half feet. 'No.'

'What?' Maude's eyes were as large as the gold baubles attached to her earlobes.

'I said no. You're staying here. Just like Dr Alexander wants.'

'Well,' she huffed. 'I never dreamed you'd—'

Maude's face turned green, and this time Gideon grabbed a fresh basin and tucked it under her mouth.

The moment her heaves stopped, she settled herself in bed, looking regal in spite of her pasty color. 'I suppose I can stay tonight. I certainly hope the bed will be softer than this one.'

'The nurses will do their best to accommodate you,' Gideon assured her, well aware that the staff would be hard-pressed to satisfy their newest patient. 'We'll start with blood work now. Your X-rays will be taken first thing in the morning. Until then you're only allowed water. No food.'

'I didn't get my dessert,' Maude informed him. 'I never miss my sweet.'

Sally choked back a cough. Gideon cleared his throat and refocused his gaze on Mrs Patterson. 'I'm sorry, but you will today.'

He exited the room with Sally on his heels. Scribbling his orders, he asked, 'Who's the surgeon on call?'

'Dr Miller.'

'Hopefully she won't need his services tonight.' He signed his name with brisk motions. 'Administer the morphine, schedule her X-rays, then get her comfortable upstairs.'

'Do you really think that's possible? To get her comfortable?' the blonde asked, quirking one eyebrow.

Gideon handed her the chart and grinned. 'Probably not, but do your best.'

'Something tells me it won't be good enough,' she mourned.

Gideon headed for the closest stairwell and bounded up three flights to pay another official visit.

'How are you doing today, John?' he asked upon entering the room.

The grizzled carpenter clicked through the television channels with his remote control and grimaced. 'Bored stiff, Doc.' He chuckled at his own joke.

Gideon stood next to the bed and the occupant waved his hand across his face. 'Wow, Doc! No offense, but have you been visitin' some ladies you shouldn't be? Or did you meet a skunk somewhere?'

Gideon smiled. 'Pretty bad, huh?'

John nodded.

'Truth is, I have a patient who enjoys her perfume.'

'Boy, Doc. If I was you, I'd take a shower quick. Your outfit's prob'ly ruined, too. Better be careful around matches. Those fumes could ignite.'

Gideon laughed. 'I'll remember. By the way, I have good news. You don't have meningitis or encephalitis.'

'I can go home now?'

He shook his head, hating to dash John's hopes. 'Not yet. I should have the rest of the results in a few days. In the meantime I want to continue the antibiotics.'

'So I can't get rid of this?' John raised his hand with its intravenous line.

'Sorry. It won't be much longer.' Gideon decided not to lower the man's spirits further with the news that if he *did* have Lyme Disease, as suspected, he'd be stuck in the hospital with IV antibiotics for at least two weeks. No point in worrying over possibilities.

'Are the nurses taking good care of you?'

'Can't complain.' John motioned Gideon closer, his grin sporting several missing teeth. In a whisper, he added, 'I 'specially like those bedtime backrubs. An old bachelor like me could get real spoiled, if ya know what I mean.'

Gideon laughed, and patted the man's striped-pajama-clad shoulder. 'Enjoy them while you can. I'll see you tomorrow.'

He visited Peter Coffman next. The elderly gentleman responded to Gideon's questions with very weak nods, but Gideon had high hopes that he would recover from his bout with endocarditis. Natalie's culture and drug sensitivity report had confirmed the treatment regimen he'd initiated earlier.

Satisfied with his patients' conditions for the night, he meandered through the corridors toward the doctors' entrance and peered through the plate glass before leaving the building. Streetlights illuminated the night in eerie patterns as the rain fell in a steady drizzle. Resigned to a drenching, he hunched his shoulders and darted outside to his car.

A quiet house greeted him ten minutes later—a gentle reminder of Katie's plans to attend a movie with her new friend, Sara. Although he wanted her to become acquainted with kids her own age, he missed hearing a cheery voice welcome him home.

Standing in the center of the kitchen, he fantasized about walking in to a wife who looked remarkably like Natalie. She'd throw her arms around his neck and welcome him with a kiss that promised things to come. A couple of children would run in, hug his legs and yell 'Daddy' at the top of their little lungs.

Gideon grinned.

But the house's stillness intruded on his dream, and the vision faded into reality. He was alone; no one was there to greet him. The pitter-patter he heard was nature at work, not the sound of little feet, and the only things clinging to him were his damp clothes and the still powerful scent of gardenias.

Spending an evening alone wasn't intolerable, but

the floral odor definitely had to go. He strode toward the bathroom as he unbuttoned his shirt, then shrugged it off and tossed it into a waiting laundry basket.

With water spraying over his soapy body, his mind raced back to the shocking information he'd received two days ago.

He, Gideon Alexander, was responsible for Natalie's latest professional setback. She might think he was only indirectly involved, but he knew better. If he'd accepted her father's money he wouldn't have squeezed more concessions out of Bill Burns, and she would now be working in a newly remodeled, re-equipped microbiology lab.

He was supposed to *help* her achieve success, not hinder her. If Harrison Pike learned about this, Gideon could kiss his own dreams goodbye.

There had to be something he could do. Just as one small piece of information had clarified Dr Pike's motives, one good idea could solve Natalie's deadlock with administration.

Toweling off, he revised his preconceived opinions. His 'spoiled rich kid' label no longer fit; 'determined' and 'independent' were more appropriate adjectives for someone intent on overcoming her limitations on her own.

He'd debated whether he should allow his sister to form a friendly attachment to Natalie, but his sister had been so excited at the prospect he hadn't had the heart to say no. He'd never planned to use Katie as a means to help him become Natalie's mentor; perhaps if he'd been more cold and calculating he would have.

Fate had stepped in, and if the situation worked to his advantage then so be it. Eventually everyone—including Dr Pike—would be happy.

He padded across the hallway to his bedroom, a thick blue towel wrapped loosely around his hips. After pulling on a blue knit shirt and gray gym shorts, he settled into his favorite chair with the latest *New York Times* crossword puzzle book. Whenever he had a problem he couldn't sort out he'd concentrate on something totally different and the answer would often come to mind.

He completed one page, then started another. The solutions came easily, and his pencil scratched across the newsprint without pause.

An idea formed, then another. After bolting toward Katie's desk, he sat down, grabbed a notepad, and jotted several one-word notes. When he'd filled the page he leaned back in the chair to review what he'd written. A slow grin of satisfaction crept across his face.

One of his plans would help Natalie. He knew it.

# CHAPTER FIVE

'You're quiet today,' Karen told Natalie as Monday crept to a close.

'Yeah, I guess so. Must be the rainy weather.' Natalie slid a tray of Petri dishes into the incubator before she pulled out another set and closed the door.

'You're not moping about our funding-cut, are you?'

'Heavens no.' Natalie shook her head for emphasis as she sat on a stenographer's chair and readjusted the beam from the high-intensity desklamp. 'I've been trying to come up with an alternative, but nothing's coming to mind.'

'Don't give up. Remember how hard you worked to get extra help for us? It took a long time, but your efforts paid off,' Karen remarked as she dipped a slide into the violet staining jar.

'True,' Natalie replied, remembering how she'd pestered Jim for months before he had agreed to provide a part-time tech. Her gains at St Mark's were few and far between, but they were still improvements, so she couldn't get discouraged. The magical moment when she could call her father to gloat over her own achievements would come. It had to.

She opened a set of colourful agar plates in front of her. The fluorescent green bacterial growth with its characteristic grape-like odor immediately caught her attention, and experience told her its identity. This young fellow definitely had a pseudomonas infection—

another typical case of summertime 'swimmers' ear'.

'If our work doesn't slack off soon,' she continued, thinking of the recent influx of cultures, 'I'll ask for more staff again.' She fell silent, her hand steady as she selected a single colony for further testing with a sterile looped wire. 'Although I don't know where we'd put another body in this oversized closet.'

'This corner's taken,' Susan, the petite part-timer who looked more like a teenager than a woman in her early twenties, chimed in. 'Although if you do find someone tall, dark and handsome, I'll be glad to share my space.'

Karen chuckled. 'Wouldn't we all?'

'I'll make a point to list those traits as part of the job requirements,' Natalie replied dryly.

Susan grinned. 'Make sure you put them at the top.'

'Experience unnecessary?' Natalie asked, finding their silly mood infectious.

'Details, details. We'll train him, won't we, Susan?' Karen winked.

'You bet.'

'Where do you propose we'll find men who fit your description?' Natalie asked. 'They're few and far between.'

'I've seen several,' Karen protested.

'Really? Name one.'

Karen glanced over her shoulder at Susan. 'Our boss, the skeptic.'

'No, really,' Natalie insisted. 'Name one.'

'I realize handsome is a relative term,' Karen mentioned, 'but I can't believe you've forgotten Dr Alexander.'

Not hardly.

Knowing her co-worker's penchant for teasing,

Natalie pretended to consider him with nonchalance. 'Oh, him.'

Karen shook her head. 'For heaven's sakes, the man could pose for a romance novel. I think you've been in swimming pools too long—your brain is starting to float.'

'Okay, okay. I'll admit Gid—er, Dr Alexander fits in that category. Satisfied?'

'Do I dare ask what category you're referring to?' a deep male voice asked.

Mortified by Gideon's presence at a most inopportune moment, Natalie knocked over a stack of culture plates. The hand-sized Petri dishes clattered across the table, their plastic lids flying in every direction.

'It—well—it—um—wasn't anything important,' she murmured. With her face as warm as if sunburned and her hands shaking, she hastily restored order. Thank goodness she hadn't mixed two patients' specimens together by her clumsiness.

'No, nothing important,' Karen repeated. 'It was good, though. Nothing slanderous.'

His eyes sparkled. 'I see. Anything to do with books?'

Karen coughed.

Susan snickered.

Natalie wanted to crawl into the woodwork.

The humor in his voice and the bemused grin on his face spoke volumes. Natalie sent a glare hot enough to sterilize equipment to her subordinates.

'I think I'll be going now,' Karen said casually, pulling the vinyl dustcover over the microscope with lightning speed. 'See you tomorrow.'

'Me, too,' Susan added, following close to Karen's heels.

'Lively crew, aren't they?' he commented after they'd disappeared.

'They do make the day interesting,' Natalie admitted. She straightened her shoulders and assumed an all-business attitude. 'I'm sure you didn't come to discuss my staff's personalities. How can I help you, Doctor?'

'Actually, it's more of how *I* can help *you*,' he answered.

'Oh?' She raised one eyebrow. 'What makes you think I need help?'

Gideon's gaze was direct. 'I don't see any fancy equipment in here, do you?'

'At the moment, no.' Natalie crossed her arms. 'But the possibility still exists.'

His eyes widened. 'Has Administration reversed their decision?'

'No, but—'

'Do you have another plan in mind?'

She fell silent, hating to confess that she'd run out of ideas. 'Something will come to me,' she declared. 'It always does.'

'Until then, would it hurt to listen for a few minutes?' he coaxed.

Giving in to his suggestion, she motioned to a three-legged stool. 'Have a seat.'

He sat. 'I've been thinking about your problem,' he began, 'and I think I've come up with a workable solution.'

'Which is?' She drummed her fingers on the counter.

'Have you considered a rental contract? I know of one plan where you'd agree to purchase a set amount of supplies and in exchange you'd receive your equipment at—'

'I'm familiar with the concept,' Natalie interrupted. 'I couldn't call myself a supervisor if I didn't know about things like leases and rental plans. Unfortunately, it isn't a viable option.'

'Why not?'

'The cost is too prohibitive. I'd spend less money if I hired a full-time person instead.' She shook her head. 'It's a good idea, but I can't justify it to the accounting people.'

'Okay. What about a straight lease?'

'Sorry,' she said, again shaking her head. 'The minimum contract is for five years. By the time it ended we'd have spent twice the amount of the original purchase price.'

'How about a used instrument?'

'I found one,' she admitted, 'but the administrative board won't buy previously owned equipment. They refuse to risk getting someone else's headache.'

'That's nonsense,' Gideon exclaimed. 'All it takes is a little common sense.'

Natalie shrugged, lifting both hands in surrender. 'I'm only telling you their philosophy. I don't happen to agree with it.'

'Maybe I could convince Watson to change his mind.'

'No.'

Gideon's surprise made her wish she hadn't been so emphatic. 'No,' she repeated, this time in a more modulated tone. '*I'll* ask him to reconsider. This is my problem, not yours.'

He stroked his chin and looked thoughtful, almost as if he was debating with himself.

Curiosity made her ask, 'Any other ideas?'

The corners of his mouth turned upward, and a faint

indentation in his cheek appeared.

Natalie leaned forward, her interest piqued. So far he hadn't suggested anything she hadn't previously thought of and researched. But if he had something else in mind. . .

'What you need is someone with money who'd like to make a generous donation to the hospital for your benefit. Know anyone like that?'

She swallowed. Yes, she knew someone. Her father—who'd be delighted to perform another philanthropic gesture for his daughter. Her stomach tensed.

'Sorry. Can't help you,' she answered, avoiding Gideon's gaze. Her father's name would remain confidential.

'Maybe one of the local organizations would be interested in either donating or raising money for hospital equipment.'

Natalie thought a moment. 'I don't know,' she said slowly, frowning. 'I don't want people to just *hand* me something.'

'It isn't any different from the hospital's administrative people reading your justification and deciding to allocate the money to you,' Gideon insisted, his dark-eyed gaze fixed on hers.

'I guess not,' Natalie mused aloud, still unconvinced.

'In fact, you'll probably work harder, because you'll have to sell the public something they know nothing about, and they won't understand its benefits.'

His perspective made sense, but she still had doubts. Asking superiors for materials to perform a job was one thing, but going to the local residents resembled begging.

'I don't know. . .' she began, shaking her head. A suspicion grew and she narrowed her eyes. 'Why are you doing this for me? Respiratory Therapy is in the same predicament I am.'

Somewhat sheepish, he said, 'I really hadn't thought of them, but there isn't any reason we can't work together. I came to you first because my main interest is in infectious disease. I know how much I rely on your department.'

He reached into his coat's breast pocket and pulled out a folded piece of paper. 'Here's a list of Rocky Hills' civic organizations, along with the names and phone numbers of their current presidents.'

Natalie scanned the page's five entries. Somehow she'd lost control, in a few short seconds. 'You've been very thorough.'

'Thank my secretary. She called the Chamber of Commerce this morning and compiled the information.'

'I see.'

'I'll call a few of the people this evening. The sooner we know if their organizations will help us, the better.'

His take-charge attitude began to grate on her nerves. 'I should discuss this with Ed Higgins before you run all over town soliciting contributions. Don't you agree?'

He looked unconcerned. 'I talked to him early this afternoon. He's all for it.'

Simmering irritation now grew to a boil. She refolded the paper with deliberate movements, trying to hide the tremor in her hands caused by suppressed anger. 'You keep saying "we" and "us", but unless you have a toad in your pocket I only see *you* at work. *You've* collected names. *You've* talked to Higgins. *You'll* call members of the community. What am I supposed to do—smile and be your cheering section?'

He blinked, obviously taken aback by her accusations. 'I admit I researched a few things before I mentioned my idea. I didn't want to raise your hopes unnecessarily.'

'You didn't want to raise my hopes unnecessarily?' she parroted. A familiar surge of frustration swept over her, knocking out huge chunks of her self-control. 'Who put you in charge of protecting me or my feelings?'

Gideon's actions reminded her of someone else's—someone with whom she'd fought many battles in a personal war of independence. She hadn't moved away from Denver to exchange one dictator for another, no matter how well-intentioned he might be.

'I'm sorry. I was only trying to help,' he said, his eyes wide and his voice full of surprise.

'Help?' Natalie scoffed, jumping to her feet to pace while she seethed at the idea. 'I don't consider going over my head to Higgins as "help". You had no right to get his permission for anything concerning my department.'

He rose. 'I said I'm sorry. It won't happen again,' he said stiffly.

'You're right—it won't,' she declared, thrusting the scrap of paper at him. 'I won't beg the people of this town for what I need, and I don't care if Higgins *has* given his blessing.'

He folded his arms over his chest. 'I can't believe you're fighting this because I did some advance footwork. Footwork, I might add, that most people would appreciate.'

'I explained my position. If you weren't so overbearing, you'd understand,' she said through gritted teeth.

'I understand perfectly,' he retorted, a muscle

pulsing in the side of his cheek. 'I stepped on your ego by having an idea when you didn't.'

She stopped short. 'That's preposterous.'

'Is it?'

He squared his jaw and straightened his shoulders into a military-correct posture. Closing the small distance between them, he pointed his finger at her.

'You asked why I was doing this. Well, this is the bottom line, lady. My first concern is to my patients, and if helping you benefits them then that's what I'm willing to do. If you can't live with that, tough.'

He strode toward the door. Hesitating on the threshold, he muttered, 'Oh, hell,' before he pivoted and re-approached her.

Natalie braced herself for more harsh words, her heart racing from a fresh surge of adrenalin.

'I thought we could enjoy a working relationship. Maybe even become friends. Obviously I was wrong.'

She bit her lip.

'Since that's out of the question, it's time I left. But before I do, I want to satisfy my curiosity. . .'

There was no time to assimilate his cryptic comment, no time to imagine his intentions before he gripped her upper arms and latched his hard mouth onto hers.

The contact was electrifying.

His warm embrace surrounded her as he yanked her so close that his shirt-buttons dug into one breast. Her anger dissolved as fast as sugar in water, replaced by a kinder emotion of equal intensity.

Ignoring the obvious lack of privacy and dismissing all fears of discovery, her hands crept up his hard back. His muscles rippled under her palms as her mind concentrated on the pure magic of his lips.

Gentle fingers stroked the side of her face, sending shivers down to her toes.

Pressed against him, she tasted and smelled myriad scents that she couldn't identify singly, but together they created a masculine fragrance unique to one man. Gideon Alexander.

Time stood still until he broke the contact. 'Now I know.'

'Know what?' Natalie blinked, dazed by the experience. No one had ever kissed her senseless before, though several had tried and failed.

Her question went unanswered; he was gone.

With her thoughts whirling, she sank onto the wooden stool he'd vacated and rubbed her forehead. Her white jacket's sleeve brushed against her nose, filling it with a fresh dose of his personal scent.

Compared to the last man who'd pursued a romantic entanglement, Gideon was far ahead. He didn't need to get in Harrison Pike's good graces like Mason Campbell, the orthopedic resident aspiring to become her father's protégé.

Maybe he pities you because of your handicap.

Natalie held her breath. Was it possible? Although she couldn't totally dismiss the idea, his kiss had seemed more passionate than sympathetic. Then again, she'd been fooled before.

Her gaze fell on a familiar white square lying on the floor, and she bent over to retrieve the small piece of paper. Unfolding it, she reread the neat handwriting. The words blurred as she recalled Gideon's last accusations.

Was he right? Was she so intent on doing everything for herself that she defeated her own purpose? Was

she building her ego at the expense of the patients?
  She sighed. Self-analysis was so painful.

Breathing deeply, Gideon strode down the corridor
leading to the patient wings. Natalie Canfield Pike had
to be the most stubborn, exasperating woman he'd
ever met. No wonder Harrison had resorted to sneaky
tactics. Offering to help her was tantamount to waving
a red flag at a bull.

He'd never dreamed she'd mistake a considerate gesture for an underhanded one. He hadn't meant to
usurp her authority, only gather a few facts.

Ignoring the empty elevator, he pushed open the
door to the stairwell and bounded up the steps. Exercise was a good stress reliever, and right now he spelled
stress N-A-T-A-L-I-E.

After that little outburst, he had no idea how to
proceed. Natalie had refused his assistance so he
couldn't make Harrison happy, and the only way to
make *her* happy was to leave her alone. He was stuck
between the proverbial rock and a hard place.

At the top of the stairs he paused and ran his fingers
through his hair. If only he could solve his problems
with something as simple as an injection, a prescription
or a few stitches. Unfortunately, this was more serious
than a sore throat or torn flesh.

Kissing her had made everything worse. He could
still smell her berry fragrance on his collar, taste the
wintergreen on his lips and feel her soft skin against
his arms and chest. He hadn't expected physical sparks
to fly, but they had, and now those few moments were
etched in his memory as a most pleasurable experience.

Given the right circumstances, those embers could
easily have been fanned into open flames, but that

particular blaze would never break out. It couldn't, he decided as Harrison Pike's face loomed before him. Dishonesty didn't make for a lasting relationship.

In the meantime, he had work to do. The fire exit doors clanged shut behind him as he made his way to his nearest in-patient.

'I have good news for you today,' Gideon announced to John Carpenter a few minutes later. 'All the lab reports are back and we've found the answer.'

'No kiddin'?' John asked, sounding thrilled.

'No, I'm not. You have Lyme Disease. Our tests confirmed it.'

'Never heard of it.'

'That's not unusual,' Gideon remarked, 'although it is considered now to be the most common tick-transmitted disease in this country.'

John shook his head. 'I don't remember runnin' into any ticks.'

'I'm not surprised. The disease is more prevalent on the east and west coasts, especially during late spring and summer, but Colorado has had a few cases.'

'And I'm one of 'em.'

Gideon grinned at his patient's mournful tone. 'Yes, but now that we know what we're dealing with we can treat you more appropriately. I know you won't like it, but you have to keep your IV for two more weeks.'

'And then?'

'You'll have several weeks of oral antibiotics, but you can take those at home.' Gideon examined John's hands before he plugged his stethoscope into his ears and listened to John's chest sounds.

'So, Doc, when can I go back to work?'

Gideon poked his instrument into his jacket pocket. 'The organism causing this disease is a sneaky creature.

It can be treated, but it takes a long time. Rest is extremely important, so don't plan any strenuous projects for a while. I can't give you a definite date; we'll have to see how fast you respond to therapy.'

A nurse bustled in, carrying another intravenous fluid bag. 'I see your new medicine's arrived,' Gideon said as the woman replaced the unit on the stand with the fresh one. 'Any questions?'

'Naw. I'm just glad you figured out what was wrong.'

Gideon smiled. 'Me, too.'

His next patient wasn't as perky, although Peter Coffman *was* more alert. 'I can't take a deep breath,' the elderly man complained. 'It isn't so bad, though, if I'm sitting up.'

Gideon listened carefully to the man's heart. Shortness of breath was the most common and earliest sign of heart failure. When he'd finished, he straightened.

'I'm ordering a few tests to check your heart again,' he said. 'Don't be alarmed when you're poked and prodded during the next few hours. I understand we have a cardiology clinic tomorrow, so I'll have the specialist check you over while he's here.'

'Is something wrong?' Peter's faded brown eyes held worry.

'It's too soon to tell,' Gideon consoled him. 'Since we have an expert coming, we might as well keep him busy. Don't want him to get bored.'

A faint smile appeared on Peter's lined face. 'You're the doctor.'

Outside the room, Gideon pulled Coffman's petite, red-headed nurse aside and explained his written orders in a low voice.

'I want an EKG and chest X-ray STAT, along with cardiac enzymes, CBC, electrolytes, kidney function studies and another blood culture. Get an echocardiogram ASAP, and be sure Dr Morrison, the cardiologist, sees him first thing tomorrow.

'I also want you to watch for any signs of edema. His ankles don't look swollen now, but that could change. I want to know if it does.'

She nodded. 'Heart failure?'

'Let's hope not,' Gideon replied grimly, heading for his last patient.

He'd only appeared in Mrs Patterson's doorway when the woman began her diatribe. 'It's about time you arrived, Doctor. I think you should know I've waited most of the day for my silly old X-ray. I thought I was supposed to have it done this morning.'

'Sometimes delays are inevitable. Radiology took care of you as soon as they could,' he soothed.

'Do you have a report yet? I'd like to leave. A person just can't get any rest here, and the food is positively horrid. Broth and gelatin just won't do.'

Gideon cleared his throat. 'Until your gallbladder improves, you'll be eating very lightly. There isn't any indication of stones, so until we get a lab report we'll treat you for a bacterial infection.'

'Which means?'

'You'll receive a lot of antibiotics. If you don't improve in a few days, we'll consider surgery.'

'Surgery?' she screeched, her eyes owlish.

'Only if the drug therapy doesn't produce results,' he emphasized.

'Surgery?' she repeated weakly. 'I never dreamed. . .'

'As I said, let's give the medicine a chance. I'll check in on you tomorrow.' Without giving her another opportunity to complain, he left.

Gideon drove home, eager for a quiet evening and several hours of mindless activity. The less he thought about his predicament with Natalie, the better.

'Is she coming?' Katie asked, the minute he walked through the back door.

'Oh, Katie, I forgot to ask her,' he answered truthfully.

'I'll call her. Maybe she hasn't eaten yet.' Katie rushed to the telephone and picked up the receiver.

Gideon tugged it out of her hand and dropped it in its hook. 'I don't think it's a good idea. Not tonight.'

'Why not?'

He rubbed his face. 'Just take my word for it.'

Katie's dark eyes narrowed. 'Did you two argue?'

He shrugged. 'In a manner of speaking.'

'Over what?'

'You wouldn't understand.' He grabbed a celery stick from a bowl of sliced vegetables and bit into it.

'Try me. I'm not a child.' With her chin tilted, she looked every bit as stubborn as Natalie, heaven help him.

He bowed to the inevitable. 'I had an idea for a way she could get some equipment. She didn't want my help and we exchanged words. Now you know, so can we talk about something else?'

She nodded, and he took his place at the table. Relaxed by the good food and light conversation, he was totally unprepared for her next question.

'Have you ever thought of getting married?'

His fork paused in midair. 'Tired of looking after me already?'

'That's not it,' she protested, her ponytail swinging as she shook her head. 'I just wondered if you wanted to get married. Mom said you didn't date much, even in medical school.'

'She told you that?' he asked, incredulous.

Katie nodded. 'Yeah. Why didn't you?'

'I dated,' he insisted. 'I took my schooling seriously, but I saw a few women on a social basis.'

'Did you like them?'

He shrugged. 'I asked them out, so I must have.'

'Not enough to marry them, though?'

'You're right.'

'Do you want to get married?'

'Persistent tonight, aren't we?' He quirked one eyebrow, amused by Katie's seriousness. 'To answer your question, I'm sure I will when the right woman comes along.'

'What are you looking for? Wife-wise?'

'If you're thinking to screen applicants, think again. I can handle it by myself.' He leaned back in his chair. 'Since you're so concerned, what traits do *you* think I should be looking for my future, as yet nameless wife to have?'

Katie's response was quick, as if she'd already thought it out. 'Pretty, smart, someone who likes the things you do. She can't be a doormat, either. I need to like her, and vice versa.'

'Of course.' He grinned. 'Do you have someone in mind?'

'I did.'

'Oh?' Gideon quickly ran through the women he knew his sister had met, and just as quickly discarded them. Natalie, however, remained in his mind.

'Yeah, I did. At least until you picked a fight with her.'

'I didn't pick a fight with her. It just came up.'

'Whatever.' Her eyes became wide, as if something had occurred to her. 'You thought of her too, didn't you? Are you going to apologize?'

He ignored her first question. 'What for?'

Katie shrugged. 'I don't know. Maybe you were too pushy; big brothers have a tendency to be like that. Then again, someone has to make the first move.'

He scooted away from the table to stand, the truth of Katie's comment too close for comfort. 'In that case, I move that we end this conversation. I'll even wash the dishes tonight.'

Katie declined. 'That's okay. It isn't like I have something else to do. Besides, when you put things away I can't find them again.'

He hugged her. 'I'm sorry this evening didn't turn out the way you wanted.'

'Don't worry about it.' Breaking away, she tilted her head to meet his gaze. 'If she *does* want to go out sometime—for girl-stuff—can I?'

Although he doubted it would happen, he couldn't dash Katie's hopes. 'Sure. Just because Natalie and I disagree doesn't mean you two can't be friends.'

Katie smiled. 'Thanks.'

He chucked her on the chin, his spirits rising since he'd made her happy. 'Anytime.'

Gideon meandered into the living-room, unrolled the nightly newspaper and headed for his favorite chair. Maybe he had been pushy, although he hadn't intended to be. It was a sad day when a man couldn't do something thoughtful without getting accused of dastardly motives.

He'd glanced at the headlines when the door-bell rang.

Expecting Katie to dart through the house at

breakneck speed to answer, he called out, 'I'll get it.'

A few steps later Gideon flung open the door, and his jaw immediately dropped at the sight of his visitor.

There, on the porch, stood a bedraggled-looking Natalie.

# CHAPTER SIX

NATALIE'S resolve failed the minute Gideon opened the door. Apologizing had seemed like a good idea while she was walking through the evening mist, but now she wasn't so sure. It certainly would have been easier to carry out her self-appointed task if he'd looked less like a judge about to condemn a felon to life imprisonment.

Get it over with, her inner voice instructed.

She took a deep breath and spoke in a rush. 'I'm sorry for being such a pill, earlier. I was so caught up in trying to prove myself that I lost sight of the most important thing—the patients. You had a very good suggestion, and I shouldn't have been so quick to dismiss it. At any rate, I'm sorry.'

Her shoulders slumped with relief. It was over. Without waiting for his response, she bounded down the three porch steps, her tennis shoes making soggy noises as her feet hit the concrete.

'Wait,' he called as he stepped outside, the door closing behind him with an audible click.

Natalie paused. Slowly, with great trepidation, she pivoted to face him.

'Apology accepted.' A glimmer of a smile appeared.

She nodded once, her own smile tentative. As his dimple became more pronounced giddiness washed over her, and her grin matched his own. She remembered a line at the end of an old movie: 'And all was right with the world', and she wholeheartedly concurred.

She turned toward the street, but once again his tenor voice stopped her in her tracks. 'Hold on.' Two footfalls later he stood next to her on the sidewalk, with one hand cupping her elbow and his dark hair shimmering with water droplets.

'You're getting wet,' she pointed out lamely.

He looked out at the street, then back at her. 'Where's your car?'

'At home.'

'Where's home?'

She felt her face warm. 'The other side of town. Near the shopping center.'

'Good God,' he exploded. 'That's—what—fifteen blocks away?'

'More or less.' She didn't have the heart to mention that she had counted twenty-one. 'Our city blocks are small. It's only a couple of miles.'

Gideon raised closed eyes to the sky, his lips barely moving. She thought he mentioned something about needing a keeper, but she wasn't positive. 'You can't walk back,' he declared, impaling her with his gaze. 'You'll catch pneumonia. You're already soaked. Just look at your shoes.'

Natalie didn't need to look—her feet had told her five blocks ago that her socks were completely saturated.

'I'll drive you home.'

'I can get there—'

'By yourself,' he finished. 'Yes, I know, but humor my medical sensibilities, okay?'

'All right.' In spite of her bravado, she really didn't want to walk another hour in waterlogged clothes.

'Do you make a habit of traipsing through town in the rain?' he asked as he ushered her into the house and closed the door.

'It's only misting,' she defended herself. 'I hadn't planned to go so far. It just happened.' Hating to drip on the carpeting, she waited on the entryway rug while he disappeared into another room.

She flicked a dripping lock of hair out of her eyes and caught a whiff of her fleece sweatshirt. It smelled like rain and the outdoors after a storm—a contrast to the delicious aroma of Italian seasoning. He'd obviously had something like spaghetti or lasagne for supper, while she'd created a bland grilled cheese sandwich. She shivered, the chill of her damp clothes and sopping feet colliding with the warmer air inside.

Gideon walked back into the hall, carrying a cream-colored fisherman's knit sweater, socks, sandals and a thick bathtowel. 'Here you go,' he said, thrusting the terrycloth into her hands while he held everything else.

'Thanks.' She unfolded it and began towelling her hair dry.

'Take off the shirt.'

'Why?' she paused to ask.

He waved the garment in his hand. 'To put this on.'

'It really isn't necessary,' she protested. 'I can be home in ten minutes.'

'It's either this or you're taking a hot bath before we leave.'

'Now, see here. . .'

He came closer. 'I know you have trouble accepting suggestions, but consider this a doctor's order. You *can* follow those, can't you?'

Natalie had opened her mouth to recant her apology when she caught the teasing glimmer in his eye. 'Okay,

okay,' she said, secretly glad to comply. Dropping the towel, she stripped the sweatshirt over her head and revealed a relatively dry tube-top.

Instantly she realized her error. The form-fitting fabric hugged her curves like a second skin. The top edge had slipped dangerously low, exposing the pale flesh beneath her tan line and a tiny mole in the middle of her left breast. Goosebumps rose all over, not from the cold but from his hungry gaze.

Something inside of her begged for his touch, but common sense regained its firm grip—this was not the time or the place for a weak moment.

Grabbing his sweater, she pulled it over her head. It engulfed her, the sleeves hanging several inches past her fingertips. Pushing them above her wrists, she breathed in the woodsy scent clinging to the fibers and reveled in her new-found warmth. Knowing, also, that he too had worn it sent a tremor of excitement down her spine. 'Mmm, this is nice.'

The corners of his mouth quivered. 'Let this be a lesson—never argue with the doctor. Now the shoes.'

'My feet can last ten minutes.'

'The shoes. And the socks.'

'Oh, all right.' Exasperated at his mulish tone, she kicked off the soggy canvas footwear. Standing on one foot like a crane, and resting one hand on his forearm for balance, she peeled off one sock, then the other. 'You really are overbearing and bossy.'

'I've heard that.' He thrust a replacement pair at her, along with a pair of men's sandals. 'Put those on. They're too big, but at least they're dry.'

After she'd complied, she said, '*Now* can we go?'

His dimple appeared. 'Now we can go. Katie?' he called. 'I'm taking Natalie home.'

Katie materialized in the doorway to the living-room, a dishtowel in hand. 'Natalie's here?'

'Hi, Katie,' Natalie responded, wondering if the girl had recognized whose clothes Natalie was wearing.

'Does this mean you're getting along again?' the girl asked hopefully.

'We'll see you later,' Gideon replied firmly, evading her question. 'Don't wait up.'

Katie's smile broadened until a dimple similar to Gideon's showed in her cheek. 'I won't, big brother.'

He ushered Natalie outside to his car. 'What did you mean when you told her, "Don't wait up"?' she asked. 'You are taking me home, aren't you?'

'Yes, but I'm not leaving until you've taken care of yourself.' He slammed the door after she'd settled into the passenger seat.

The moment he got in she asked, 'Since when do you make house calls?'

'You're my very first, but don't let it go to your head. Where to?'

Natalie recited her address and gave directions. In no time at all he had parked the car in front of her apartment complex, and she pulled a keyring out of her zippered wrist pouch. 'Thanks for the ride. I can take it from here.'

He shook his head. 'Tsk, tsk. Are you trying to deprive me of a new experience?' Sounding amused, he got out of the car at the same time she did.

'Anyone ever tell you that you're singleminded?' she asked.

'Many times,' he replied. 'Shall we go in?'

Resigned to the inevitable, she hurried up the walk to the four-plex's common entrance. 'My place is near the back,' she told him, leading the way through the hall to the farthest door on the left. The turn of a key later they were inside.

'Have a seat.' She motioned to the furniture while at the same time trying to visualize the room from a stranger's perspective. Her pieces were solid and well-built, chosen for comfort and function rather than design.

Tidiness reigned except for the coffee-table, which held her half-finished cross-stitch garden scene and boxes of brightly colored threads.

The quiet gurgle of her aquarium beckoned. Dropping a few pinches of food-flakes to the waiting angel fish, she asked, 'Can I get you something to drink?'

'Maybe later,' he said, sinking into the beige-toned rocker-recliner.

'Okay.' Before she left the room, she announced, 'I won't be long.'

'No problem.'

Natalie rushed to the bathroom adjoining her bedroom. While removing her hearing-aids she opted for a hot shower—too aware of the handsome, virile man waiting a few feet away to enjoy a leisurely bath.

The moment she had finished—her skin glowing pink and her aids back in place—she dashed into the bedroom to slip on an old pair of stone-washed jeans and a novelty T-shirt that read, 'I'm a microbiologist. Don't bug me'.

Grabbing a plastic grocery sack, she stuffed in his sandals and reached for his sweater. Her haste suddenly forgotten, she held it close, nuzzled her nose in its softness, and breathed in the smell that branded it as Gideon's. With deliberate movements she folded the bulky sweater, then traced the path of the cabled design with a light touch.

For heaven's sakes, she scolded herself, act your age. She crammed the last of his apparel into the bag and left the room.

'I followed orders,' she announced when she saw him. 'Mission accomplished.'

'Glad to hear it.' He rose. 'Shall I collect my fee now, or save it for another time?'

'Fee?' Her mind went blank. What kind of payment was he expecting? She might have been putty in his arms, but surely he didn't expect. . .?

'Earlier you offered something to drink,' he reminded her.

Her breath left her. 'Oh, yes. Yes, of course. Forgive me. What would you like?'

'Something hot?'

'I have instant tea and instant spiced apple cider. No coffee—sorry.'

He raised one dark eyebrow. 'I didn't think you'd be an "instant" sort of person.'

'Why not?'

'Well, first, your job is rather time-consuming. Secondly, your cross-stitch hobby requires painstaking effort, and I know it takes weeks and sometimes months before you see progress with your projects.'

She grinned, shrugging. 'Chalk it up to a quirk in my personality—although I'm glad I can keep you guessing. So which would you prefer?'

'Apple cider.' He cocked his head and sniffed the air as he followed her into the kitchen. 'Speaking of guessing, what is that good smell?'

She pointed to a simmering pot filled with a rich red liquid. 'Winter mulberry potpourri. It's my favorite, although I switch to cranberry once in a while. Reminds me of Christmas, but then with my name being Natalie it isn't surprising.'

'I'd forgotten Natalie means 'born at Christmas tide'. Were you born in December?'

'December twenty-fifth. At 12:01 a.m. How did you get your name? Gideon is rather unusual.' She placed two mugs of water into the microwave, set the timer and pushed 'start'.

'My dad traveled a lot, and was in another state when I was born. Mom worked in a motel, and every room had a Bible donated by the Gideon Society. Since they hadn't decided on a name, when the time came to list one on the birth certificate she wrote Gideon.'

'How interesting,' she exclaimed.

'Yeah. It could have been worse. She might have thought of "Homer" instead,' he joked.

Natalie laughed as she handed him a steaming cup of apple cider. 'You don't look like a Homer now, and I'm sure you didn't then,' she said, picturing him as an infant.

'How long have you worn hearing-aids?' he asked.

'I was a little older than Katie at the time,' she said, leading him toward the polished walnut dining-table and motioning to a cushioned chair.

'An accident?' He sat at her right hand.

She shook her head. 'I was at a girlfriend's sixteenth birthday party when I noticed I couldn't hear what my friends were saying over the background music. I thought it was one of the aftereffects of an ear infection, but it never improved.'

She took a deep breath. 'My parents took me to ENT and audiology specialists and I was diagnosed with otosclerosis, which, as you know, is a bone overgrowth in the inner ear that prevents sounds from being conducted. I had corrective surgery, but it wasn't entirely successful. I also had some eardrum damage, so I began wearing aids.'

'You don't need any of the special equipment for the hearing-impaired?'

'The television and telephone have amplifiers and the phone flashes a light when it rings. Other than that, I have the same things you do. My dad, of course, wanted to buy every gadget on the market.' She paused before continuing, 'He was—and is—very protective.'

Gideon nodded. 'A common reaction in parents who have a child with a chronic disease.'

'My brother needed glasses and he didn't get smothered. Hearing-aids shouldn't be considered any differently.'

He shrugged. 'I agree. Maybe there were other variables. Are you the youngest?'

She wrinkled her nose. 'Yes.'

'Being the baby in the family probably contributed to your so-called "smothering". Did your mom treat you the same way?'

Natalie pictured her mother. 'No, she expected me to be independent, but Dad usually overruled her. He even went so far as to buy me a lab position in Denver. When I discovered what he'd done I left town without telling anyone and came here.'

Gideon's eyebrows became one line. 'He *bought* a position?'

She nodded, deciding to give only the bare facts and keep her father's identity a secret for a little longer. 'Made a huge donation to the hospital so I'd get the job.'

'That doesn't surpri— Er, I mean, I'm surprised he would do something so obvious.'

'It wasn't common knowledge. I found out by accident. Needless to say, I was devastated. My own father thought I couldn't get a job without his help.'

'Now you're trying to prove yourself?'

'Yeah. That's probably why I reacted like I did when you'd worked everything out without me. I felt like—'

'I had taken over,' he finished. 'I understand, but, Natalie, I was only trying to help.'

'I know.'

His gaze bored into hers. 'What have you decided to do?'

Natalie took a deep breath and ran her index finger around the top of her mug. 'I thought we'd call the names on the list. That is, if you're still willing.'

He rubbed his chin. 'No, I don't think so,' he began slowly.

Disappointed, she tugged her hair over one ear. She'd hoped to learn if their attraction had any substance, any depth, and working together would have been a great opportunity to do so. 'Okay,' she said stiffly.

He reached over and covered her hand with his. 'I'd be happy to do whatever I can, but I think you're as anxious to prove your capabilities to yourself as you are to your father.'

She thought a moment. 'I guess I am.'

'Then I can't stand in your way. I will, however, be available whenever you want to bounce an idea around or get a second opinion. Is it a deal?'

How thoughtful he was to recognize something she hadn't realized herself. Her eyes burned. She glanced at the ceiling and blinked her eyes. Once composed, she addressed him with a weak smile. 'Deal.'

A smile transformed his face, and she was acutely

aware of his fingers tracing circles on the top of her hand. His gentle touch comforted, yet sent excitement pulsing through her arm. Like a magnet drawn to steel, she couldn't pull her hand away. Nor did she want to.

He hadn't changed out of his earlier attire, although his sleeves were rolled to just below his elbow and the shirt-buttons at his throat had been undone.

His forest smell wafted toward her, mingling with the mulberry fragrance as perfectly as if it had been formulated into a new perfume.

'Now that you know what I'm trying to do with my life,' she began lightly, 'what about you?'

'As you're already aware, my interest lies in infectious diseases. Eventually I want to enter a program in that field.'

This time his talk of leaving town sent a sharp pain of disappointment and loss through her mid-section. She tried to disregard it by asking, 'How did you get the bump on your nose?' She reached to touch the spot without thinking.

'Broke it.'

She gave him a tell-me-something-I-don't-know look. 'In a fight?'

He grinned. 'What do you think?'

Natalie studied him, her eyes narrowed. 'Even if your hands weren't important to your work, you don't seem the type to use fists.'

'Very good, Miss Canfield. Actually, a windstorm blew in and I went outside to nail down a few loose shutters. I was on the last one when an extra strong gust blew it out of my hands and into my nose.'

'Ouch.' She winced in a sympathy pain.

'I believe I said a much stronger four-letter word,' he remarked. 'In fact, my younger brother Tom was quite impressed with my sixteen-year-old vocabulary.'

'Were you home alone?'

He shook his head. 'Mom was inside with Katie—she was only a baby and sick at the time. She wanted us to wait until she could help, but Tom and I were the men of the house, so we didn't.'

Natalie thought back to the family snapshot she'd seen on his desk. No wonder Gideon looked more serious than his siblings—he'd taken on responsibilities more suitable to an adult.

At that moment the cuckoo clock's door popped open and a brightly colored wooden bird skidded out of its house as the hourly song played. Before the echo from the tenth bong died, it had slid back into its home and the door had closed with a snap.

'I'd better go,' Gideon remarked, squeezing her hand as if reluctant to turn it loose. 'Katie has an extremely active imagination, and if I'm not home soon she'll imagine all sorts of things. I can't lecture her on social and moral responsibility if I don't follow the same rules.'

Natalie smiled. 'Of course.'

He rose. 'Katie would like to chat with you sometime.'

Natalie followed him to the door. 'How about after our next practice?'

'I'll tell her. She'll be excited.' He paused at the threshold and held her shoulders with both hands. 'I'm glad we worked things out, Natalie.'

'Me, too,' she said softly, her nerves fluttering with expectation as he lowered his head.

His kiss came—a light brush on her lips. ''Night.'

'Goodnight,' she echoed to the closing door, her spirits a little let down by his platonic peck. Yet she couldn't complain. For some inexplicable reason she was certain they'd passed a crucial test in their relationship.

Gideon drove home on autopilot. It had taken every bit of his willpower to keep from kissing her until they both ran out of air, especially after seeing her in that tiny scrap of material. He never should have indulged himself the first time—it had been like waving a cigarette under the nose of someone struggling to quit his nicotine habit.

He also realized something else—he could look at Natalie without seeing Harrison Pike looming in the background. Tonight his admiration for her had changed into caring—caring that she obtain both her professional and personal goals.

Caring was dangerous. It led to love, and under the circumstances he couldn't succumb to that emotion. Love demanded total honesty, which he couldn't give. As it was he'd almost blurted a remark about her father's character that a casual acquaintance couldn't possibly have made. At least she hadn't noticed his slip.

He'd have to be much more careful. He couldn't ruin things now.

'So you're experiencing some intestinal problems,' Natalie said to the two ladies in the labratory's waiting-room the next morning. She had asked to be notified when patients with a similar complaint arrived, for whatever reason, hoping to ferret out clues.

'You can say that again,' Mrs Davidson announced, the lines in her middle-aged face pronounced. 'I've swallowed every anti-diarrheal medicine available for the last ten days, and nothing works.'

'My four- and six-year-olds have the same problem.' Mrs Vincent's dark head nodded in agreement. 'This flu has hit a lot of people.'

'How long has your family been ill?' Natalie asked. Her part-time help had called in sick that morning and Natalie hoped that the ailment would run a quick course—she needed her.

'About five days,' Mrs Vincent said. 'I certainly hope these tests will show something. This business is getting old, real fast.'

'I understand. Have you eaten anything different lately? Tried new recipes or ingredients, perhaps?'

Both women shook their heads. Natalie handed them the stool specimen containers along with typed instructions for collection and handling. 'Bring the samples in as soon as you can.'

She walked into her laboratory and a harried-looking Karen thrust the phone at her. 'For you,' she announced.

Amanda Evans, one of the county public health nurses, was on the line. 'We've had reports of some sort of gastrointestinal outbreak in the community. Can you tell me anything about it?'

'Only that we're seeing a massive amount of cultures from both young and old.'

'Have you found anything noteworthy?'

'I'm afraid not,' Natalie admitted. 'If I do, I'll let you know.'

'Thanks,' Amanda replied.

Natalie spent the rest of her morning mulling over the latest epidemic. Could she have overlooked something?

No, she decided. She'd checked and double-checked, and none of the media plates had shown any disease-causing bacteria. Yet something was responsible, and she voiced her concern at the monthly Infection Control Meeting a few hours later.

'I've had a tremendous influx of stool examinations this past week, and the numbers aren't dwindling. Any ideas?' she asked the assembled group.

'You're the one interested in infectious diseases, Gideon,' remarked Dr Halston, a urologist in his early forties. 'What do you think?'

Gideon twirled a pencil between his fingers. 'I admitted two patients from Resthaven Nursing Home this morning suffering from the same problem along with severe dehydration. It could be anything from a parasite to a virus.'

'I doubt everyone has been out of the country, so we can eliminate parasites from the picture,' Dr Halston commented. 'And if our bacterial cultures are negative then all that's left to consider is some kind of virus.'

'It's too early for flu season—especially for it to be so widespread.' Gideon addressed Natalie. 'Maybe we should look into ordering a few viral cultures?'

She nodded. 'I'll make arrangements for some of the samples to be sent to our reference lab.'

'Good.'

'What about food poisoning?' a nurse asked.

'Since nursing home patients are affected as well as the general public, I doubt it,' Gideon interjected. 'Has anyone talked to the people at the Health Department?'

'One of their nurses called me this morning,' Natalie replied. 'They're as puzzled as we are. I've also been compiling data on the patients, but I haven't discovered any links yet.'

'Then we keep looking,' Gideon remarked.

After the meeting disbanded, he followed Natalie out of the conference room. 'I'll request those cultures on my two nursing home patients—Ida Rutherford and Vincent Carr. To be honest, I'm rather concerned about them. They're both in their nineties and their immune systems aren't the greatest. They can't fight off a serious infection.'

'I understand,' Natalie said. 'By the way, why are you transferring Peter Coffman, the endocarditis patient, today? I thought he was doing well.'

'He was, for a while. But he's showing signs of heart failure now, and the cardiologist thinks a valve replacement is in order. How's your other project going?' he asked, changing the subject.

Natalie grimaced. 'I've talked to nearly everyone on the list, but haven't had any promising responses. Two of the organizations could make small donations, but the total wouldn't come close to what I'd need. Two others are already involved in community service projects and don't have the manpower to take on another venture.' She let out a deep breath. 'I'll call the last person as soon as I can spare a few minutes.'

'I've been thinking,' he began. 'Could I borrow the file with your justifications? I might come up with another idea.'

'Sure. I'll send it to your office right away.'

'Do you have time for a cup of coffee?'

She shook her head. 'I'd love to say yes, but I've got tons of work waiting for me.'

'Where are your two comediennes?' he teased.

'Comediennes?' Natalie asked, puzzled. 'Oh, you mean Karen and Susan. Actually, I only have one today. And Karen leaves—' she checked her watch '—in about thirty minutes. I'll take a raincheck, though.'

'Fair enough.'

Natalie spent the next few hours in a frenzy of activity. It seemed that for every culture sample she processed, two more took its place. When the flood of specimens slowed to a trickle, she took time out for a phone call to the last name on Gideon's list of possible benefactors.

Unfortunately Doug Magnus was as discouraging as the others. 'I'm sorry, Natalie. I'd like to help you, but our group is committed to raising funds right now for a kid with leukemia. I wouldn't feel right funneling money toward another program—although I'm sure yours is worth it.'

'By all means, you have to help her and her family,' Natalie assured him.

'Maybe we can do something for you next spring,' he said, obviously trying to soften his negative response. 'Call me then.'

'Thanks. I appreciate it,' Natalie replied. Surely the hospital would approve the purchase in the next fiscal year, and she wouldn't have to contact him again.

She was running through her mental checklist of last-minute tasks before her day could officially end when the hospital loudspeaker interrupted her train of thought.

'Code Blue. Room 412.'

Natalie paused. The number was familiar. She pulled the logbook closer and began riffling through the pages. Using her index finger as a guide, she scanned the last page's column of room numbers, intent on learning the person's identity.

There it was—her search over. Room 412's occupant was Ida Rutherford. Gideon's patient.

## CHAPTER SEVEN

NATALIE waited for several minutes, anxious to dash up to the fourth floor and learn the outcome firsthand. At the same time she knew that the ward staff didn't need curiosity-seekers in their way.

For the next hour she forced herself to concentrate as she double-checked her inventory. Then, unable to wait any longer, Natalie walked into the chemistry lab to find someone who might have an update.

'She didn't make it,' Phil Hollister, the lab's recently hired three-to-eleven shift supervisor, reported, over the squeal of his instrument's robotic arm. 'Did you know her?'

'No,' she replied. disappointed by the news. 'We discussed her at our Infection Control Meeting earlier today. When I heard the Code Blue announced, I was curious.'

'Her electrolytes were really messed up,' he said. 'The last potassium level we reported was in the panic range. I'm not surprised her heart gave out.'

Natalie remembered from her training that potassium was a crucial element to conducting nerve impulses. Too much, as well as not enough, caused the heart to fibrillate.

'Thanks, Phil.' Sympathy for Ida's family and for Gideon rolled over her. How sad to lose his first Rocky Hills patient so soon after his arrival.

Returning to the familiar quiet and smells of her own lab, she laid out the file she had promised Gideon, deciding to leave it at his house since it was past his regular office hours.

By the time she had washed her hands and was ready to leave, Gideon had appeared in the doorway. His pinched mouth, tired eyes and slumped shoulders begged for comforting.

'I just heard about Mrs Rutherford,' she said, placing a palm on his arm. 'I'm so sorry.'

He raked his hair with his fingers. 'I am, too. I wanted an autopsy, but the family refused.'

'I'm not sure I'd allow one either,' Natalie remarked, recognizing a need to tread lightly. 'Ida was, after all, ninety-two years old. What would it have told you that you didn't already know?'

'The cause of this diarrheal epidemic, that's what,' he retorted. 'I've admitted two more patients, and pediatrics has nearly all of its beds filled with kids experiencing the same problem. I'd rather not have them all die before we find an answer.'

Natalie took no offense at his sharp tone. His muscles tensed under her fingertips and she stuck her hands in her lab coat pockets.

'You can't save everyone,' she reminded him.

'No, but I can sure as hell try.'

'I'm sure you did everything possible.'

'Did *you*?' His coal-dark gaze turned upon her.

'What are you talking about? I didn't have anything to do with—' Understanding dawned. 'I can only report what I see, Gideon.'

'You're sure you haven't missed some weird strain of salmonella?'

Natalie held onto her temper. 'I'm positive.'

'What about—?'

'Gideon,' she interrupted, as patiently as possible,

'I can give you a list of all the organisms I've ruled out.' She strode toward the incubator and flung open a door. Pulling out a rack of agar plates, she handed them to him. 'There's nothing here except normal flora. Look for yourself.'

He rubbed his forehead. 'I'm sorry. I'm sure you're right. But there has to be something we've missed.'

'I don't know what it would be.' At the sight of his furrowed brow, she added, 'I'll keep working on it.'

Pointing to the folder on the countertop, he asked, 'Is this for me?'

She nodded. 'I couldn't deliver it to your office so I thought I'd drop it by your house this evening when I bring Katie home. Take it now, if you'd like.'

'Thanks.' Picking up the folder, he headed for the door. 'Have a good time tonight.'

'We will,' she promised.

The moment Natalie opened the buffet-style restaurant's doors, delicious smells surrounded her. Her stomach grumbled in anticipation.

'Gideon tells me that you're interested in a medical career,' Natalie remarked, after she and Katie had filled their plates from the food bar. 'Any ideas which field you'd like to study?'

Katie smiled. 'No, but I am joining the high school's Medical Explorer Club. They have different speakers each month, so hearing them should help me decide which field is right for me. The first meeting is coming up in a few weeks.'

'You don't want to be a doctor, like Gideon?' Natalie grinned.

'I don't know,' Katie answered, her fork poised over her Salisbury steak. 'It's an awfully big responsibility.

I mean, people's lives depend on you.'

'Lots of medical staff directly affect the patients—not just the physicians. Lab techs, pharmacists, respiratory therapists, nurses—the list goes on and on.' Natalie salted her baked potato before taking a bite. 'Although I must admit, the doctor bears the brunt of accountability.'

'Some people are just naturals at handling all the stress. People like my brother.'

'He's always carried a load, hasn't he?'

Katie nodded. 'Mom told me over and over that she didn't know what she would have done if she hadn't had Gideon. I know he helped us a lot.'

'Was your mother sick for long?' Natalie asked.

Katie looked thoughtful. 'She wasn't doing very well the last few years, but after she got pneumonia in March she never really recovered. Gideon wouldn't say anything, but I could tell he was worried.'

Natalie wasn't surprised. Being the man of the house, and a doctor too, he would have been concerned about his mother's condition. 'I'll bet he came home whenever he could.'

Katie nodded, swallowing before she answered. 'He'd even planned to move us with him when he started his practice. He and Mom talked for hours about finding one in the mountains because she loved the scenery. For some reason, right before he finished his residency, he decided to come to Rocky Hills.' Katie's mood became pensive.

Natalie filed the information away in her memory. Gideon seemed too dedicated to his family to change long-held plans. Something drastic must have happened to influence his decision. Katie, however, wasn't the one to offer any insight.

'It all worked out, I guess. At least he was home when she died.' The teen sipped her soda.

'And you moved here with him.'

'Yeah. Rocky Hills isn't as bad as I'd first thought.' The Alexander trademark dimple appeared. 'It kinda grows on you.'

Natalie smiled. 'It sure does.'

'Why did you choose a lab career?'

Natalie thought a minute. 'I was going through a hard time with my hearing in high school, and I shied away from people. In the process I discovered that I enjoyed analytical and scientific subjects, so I earned my college degree in microbiology and entered a lab internship program.'

'Did you have medical people in your family, too?'

Natalie carefully selected her words. 'My father's a doctor.'

'No kidding? What kind?'

'An orthopedic surgeon.' Trying to avoid further discussion, she added, 'My brother is a lawyer and my sister is a school district superintendent. My mom sells real estate.'

'Cool. I bet she sees all kinds of fancy houses—like the ones in magazines.'

Natalie smiled at her exuberance. 'Yes, she does.'

Katie pushed away her nearly empty plate of food. 'That was delicious. I'm glad we waited to eat until after practice.'

'Me, too. I never could swim very well on a full stomach.'

'Sara says you're a fabulous swimmer. Did you really set a pool record when you were twelve?'

Natalie nodded. 'I worked my tail off for months. In fact, everyone teased me about growing gills.

But it was worth it.' The thrill of knowing she'd been the best of the best, for even a short period of time, had kept her going when ear infections had interfered with her training and discouragement had taken hold.

She glanced at her watch. 'I suppose we'd better go, before Gideon thinks I've kidnapped you.'

Katie sighed. 'I guess. I have an essay to write for my English class, and it's due tomorrow.'

As Natalie parked in the Alexander driveway Katie commented, 'Gideon must have been called to the hospital. His car's gone.'

Fighting her disappointment, since she'd wanted to get his opinion concerning the file he'd taken, Natalie replied in a light tone, 'A doctor's work is never done. Will you be okay by yourself? Would you like me to stay?'

'I'll be fine. Thanks for asking, though.'

'If you're ever worried about being alone, you can call me anytime—day or night. I won't mind.'

'I appreciate it. Oh, I wanted to ask you—my birthday is at the end of next month, and I wondered if you'd like to come to my party? Gideon said I could plan whatever I wanted, as long as it wasn't too wild.' She grinned, her freckles adding to her pixie-ish appearance.

'I wouldn't miss it for anything,' Natalie replied.

Katie leaned across the seat and hugged her, her ponytail brushing against Natalie's cheek. 'Great.'

Natalie watched Katie walk inside before she drove away. Somehow, and in such a short space of time, both Alexanders had wiggled into a special place in her heart.

\*　　\*　　\*

Expecting another busy day at his office, considering the town's epidemic, Gideon made his morning rounds the next day as quickly as possible. John Carpenter was making slow but steady progress, and would be discharged soon. Mrs Patterson, however, was another story.

'You aren't responding as well as I'd hoped,' Gideon told the plump lady. 'Your gallbladder has to come out.'

'I want another opinion,' Maude stated.

Having anticipated her request, he replied, 'I've already made arrangements for Dr Miller, one of our surgeons, to review your case and visit with you today. If he agrees with me about surgery, he'll schedule you as soon as possible.'

'We'll see.' Maude crossed her arms as she narrowed her eyes. 'How do I know you're not telling me this so the hospital can milk more money out of me?'

Gideon pursed his lips to hold back a cynical laugh. If she only knew how every nurse on the floor had begged for her speedy discharge. Some had even offered to take up a collection to send her elsewhere. 'You're still having pain, aren't you?'

'Yes, but I only need something stronger.'

He stifled a sigh. 'Pain is your body's way of telling you there's a problem. Popping pills isn't the answer. Surgery is.'

'Oh, all right.' Maude threw up her hands. 'Since I can't leave until you people remove half of my insides, let's get it over with.'

Refusing to rise to her baited remark, Gideon left to check on Vincent Carr. The old man's condition hadn't deteriorated since his last round, although there had been several times during the past night when

Gideon had thought the mysterious illness would claim another victim.

His long stride quickly covered the block to his consultation rooms. After greeting his staff, he hurried to his private office and pressed the telephone keypad with a number from memory.

'Max?' he said into the receiver. 'Gideon.'

'It's good to hear from you, buddy,' Maxwell Nelson replied. 'Mary and I were just talking about you last night.'

'Good things, I hope.' Gideon leaned back in his chair, picturing his classmate and new wife. He'd met Mary during his rotation on Geriatrics, and had even taken the petite nurse out a few times. Romance hadn't sparked between them, but when he'd introduced her to Max it certainly had.

'You bet. Mary's anxious for you to visit. She has a friend—'

'You mean there's one I haven't met?' Gideon faked a groan.

'Afraid so,' Max chuckled. 'She won't quit until you're engaged and/or married. You haven't found someone in your neck of the woods, have you?'

A picture of Natalie flashed into his mind. 'Too busy,' he hedged. 'Anyway, I'm calling about the university's medical grant foundation. Is your dad still on the board of trustees?'

'No. He retired two months ago. If it's any consolation, I took his place.'

'That's even better,' Gideon declared. 'I need some information.' He explained Natalie's situation, finishing with, 'She could really use the money to improve her department, and I thought of the foundation. Would her request fit the guidelines?'

'The grants are mainly to furnish clinics and offices for our medical graduates, to help them establish practices in the rural part of the state. If we run the proposal through the committee and use your name and recommendation, you being an alumnus, there shouldn't be a problem. I can't promise a decision in her favor, though,' he warned.

'I don't expect you to. All I'm asking is for a chance. Do you have an application form?'

'No. Just briefly state your need in a cover letter, and include a detailed justification explaining how the patients will benefit, and so forth. You know the routine.'

With the receiver tucked between his ear and his shoulder, Gideon flipped through the pages in Natalie's file until he found the one he wanted. 'No problem. When's the deadline?'

'Two o'clock this afternoon,' Max announced.

Gideon whistled.

'You can always try for the next review.'

'Which is?'

'In six months.'

'You'll have it right away,' Gideon promised, jotting down Max's fax number. 'How soon until we know the committee's decision?'

'Next week. Maybe by the end of this one, depending on how many requests we've received.'

'Great. Thanks for the advice. I owe you one.'

'I'll collect the next time you're in town,' Max threatened good-naturedly.

Gideon broke the connection and immediately punched the number for the laboratory.

'I'm sorry, Natalie isn't in right now,' Karen reported. 'Would you like to leave a message?'

'Have her contact me as soon as possible,' he pronounced. After scribbling a letter to accompany Natalie's justifications, he instructed Barbara, his secretary, to give it top priority.

By the time he had taken a few minutes to sign the document forty-five minutes had elapsed, with no word from Natalie. Although he hated to proceed without her knowledge or approval, he had no choice. With a solidly booked schedule, he could easily lose track of time and miss the deadline. 'Fax everything. Now,' he told Barbara.

His morning passed swiftly. Gastrointestinal complaints seemed the order of the day, although he also dealt with a case of suspected hepatitis, an overweight man with chest pain and a forty-two-year-old woman with a thyroid imbalance.

After lunch he received an urgent call from St Mark's ENT specialist. 'I need you for a consult in ER. ASAP,' Dr Julie Allison said, without preamble.

'What's up?'

'Dr Larrimore just referred a woman to me, and I think you'd better see her, too.'

'I'm on my way.'

Gideon arrived a few minutes later, and was ushered into the exam room where the two physicians—one male, one female—were waiting with their patient.

As soon as the statuesque blonde saw him, she motioned him into the hallway. 'Mrs Paxton has been having nasal congestion and headaches for the past few weeks. She's been to ER several times to get some relief, but claims the medication doesn't help very long.'

'Any other complaints?'

Julie nodded. 'She has asthma, and was hospitalized

ten days ago until steroids brought it under control. To complicate things, she also has diabetes. At the moment her glucose level is four hundred and twenty-five—about three hundred points too high.'

She thrust her hands in her lab coat pockets, thumbs hanging outside. 'The right side of her face is slightly swollen and her sinuses have point-tenderness. Her fever is increasing, and with her headache and double vision I suspect intracranial complications. I'm taking her to surgery right now, to drain the right maxillary sinus, and I'd like to have you there since you're the closest thing we have to an infectious disease specialist.'

'Have you alerted the lab? We'll need stat microscopic exams.'

'Not yet. I wanted your opinion first.'

After examining Mrs Paxton, Gideon concurred with Julie's action plan. While the patient was wheeled to a suite for emergency surgery Gideon requested Natalie's presence in the anteroom before he scrubbed to assist.

When he came out later, wearing his green scrub suit and carrying the specimens Julie had collected in surgery, Natalie was waiting.

'I'll fill you in while we walk to the lab,' Gideon announced. 'Someone else could have picked up these samples, but I wanted to discuss this case with you.'

He recited Mrs Paxton's history while they hurried along the corridors, noticing how well Natalie's stride matched his own. In order to dodge hospital traffic she occasionally brushed against him, rewarding him with whiffs of her pleasant mulberry scent.

Back in her territory, Natalie took the sample and

immediately began preparing slides of the mucoid material. She treated one slide with gram-stain chemicals for bacteria while she covered another with a dye used to reveal fungal elements.

Anxious for her report, Gideon wanted to pace, but the close confines made it impossible. He sat and forced himself to relax. The room was quiet in comparison to the other areas of the lab, with only the clink of glass on glass and the sound of running water breaking the silence. The musty odor of a variety of microbes growing in concentrated amounts was familiar from his microbiology days and not totally offensive, although he preferred Natalie's special fragrance.

The moment she placed a slide under one of the microscope lenses Gideon held his breath, and drummed his fingers on the counter.

'Oh, my God,' Natalie murmured, looking through the binocular eyepieces.

'What? What do you see?' he demanded, moving closer.

'This is absolutely incredible. I've never seen anything like this before.'

'What is it?' he asked again, exasperation coloring his voice.

'The specimen is packed with a fungus of some sort. Here, have a look.' She leaned to one side.

Gideon bent down to see for himself. Although not as well versed in this area as Natalie, he knew enough to recognize the cellular structures in his sights. His heart sank. He wouldn't have minded being wrong. In fact, he would have welcomed it. Straightening, he asked, 'Can you ID it? Or at least give an educated guess?'

Natalie moved back into position and changed to a

higher power of magnification. 'I've seen this before, but we normally consider this a common fungal contaminant and dismiss it. However, since it's in a pure form, it probably *is* causing Mrs Paxton's sinus infection. As for what it is. . .' Her voice trailed off.

She scanned the slide, moving it back and forth in a systematic pattern. Reaching for a textbook on the shelf in front of her, she consulted an identification flow chart and murmured terms he recognized from a long-ago medical mycology course.

Minutes ticked by as she glanced in the microscope, then at the book, and back to the microscope. Finally he couldn't wait. 'Well?'

She leaned back, crossed her arms, took a deep breath and nibbled on her bottom lip before she looked at him. 'Mind you, I can't say for certain, but—'

'But what is it?' He was starting to sound as if he only had one sentence in his vocabulary.

'I think it's a mucor species. The material I see seems to fit the classic characteristics, but I can't be one hundred percent positive until I have a culture to work with.'

'How long?'

'If my guess is correct, it grows fairly quickly in comparison to other fungi. I'd say five to ten days.' She narrowed her eyes. 'What's wrong?'

He tried to smile. 'From an academic standpoint, you've confirmed our diagnosis of mucormycosis—or mucor for short. Less than six hundred cases have ever been reported. Good work.'

'I only call it like I see it,' she said, a small smile crossing her lips. 'But you and Dr Allison deserve most of the credit. So why aren't you excited?'

'It's a very nasty disease.'

Natalie's eyes grew wide. 'Have you had a case like this before?'

'No,' he said, reaching for the phone and pressing in the surgery's extension number. 'The university had one several years before I began my residency, and the doctors involved prepared a detailed study which was required reading.' He spoke into the receiver. 'Julie, it's confirmed.'

'I'll make arrangements to airlift her to the University Hospital,' Dr Allison replied.

'Good. I'll be there in a few minutes.' He hung up.

'What's our patient's prognosis?' Natalie asked, her forehead wrinkled.

Gideon rubbed his chin. 'I'd like to say excellent, but I can't. At one time it was always fatal, but new surgical techniques and anti-fungal drugs have improved a patient's chances. Unfortunately, the mortality rate is still thirty to eighty percent. It's worse than TB, cholera and bubonic plague—which are all treatable if caught in the early stages.'

'This fungus is so common in nature, though.'

'I know. Everyone breathes in these particles, but our immune systems are able to destroy them. In Mrs Paxton's case, her body couldn't.'

Natalie's face lit up, as if it all made sense. 'So, the steroids she used to control her asthma affected her immune response.' Her expression became puzzled. 'Lots of asthmatics take steroids. Why don't we see this disease more often?'

'There has to be the right combination of conditions. Mrs Paxton also has diabetes. From what I recall about this fungus, it loves warm, sugary environments. A diabetic's tissue—especially of one whose blood glucose level isn't within normal limits—is a wonderful place for the mucor to flourish. It can grow through the lungs, into the heart, the skull—even the brain.'

Natalie gasped. 'Is that why her headaches are so bad? It's in her brain?'

'We won't know until we get a CT scan, but it's very possible.' He rose. 'The poor woman is looking at a very long hospitalization, with multiple surgeries to clear away the infected tissue and frequent CT scans. All without any guarantee of survival.'

'We can't take care of her here?'

'Not really. She'll require massive amounts of amphotericin B. Unfortunately, while it's a powerful anti-fungal drug, it also happens to be toxic to the kidneys. Our lack of a CT machine doesn't help either. Julie Allison is also concerned that Mrs Paxton will need more extensive ENT surgery than she's capable of performing.

'Even though this is a slow-moving disease, it's considered a medical emergency—no matter what condition the patient presents. St Mark's isn't equipped to handle something as serious as this,' he finished.

'I understand.' Appearing thoughtful, Natalie said, 'I never realized something so—so *common* could be so deadly.'

'Don't forget what I said earlier. This is very rare. There are millions of people with diabetes, asthma, or a combination thereof, who never have any problem. For some reason Mrs Paxton was vulnerable, and for reasons we may never identify.'

Natalie followed him to the door. 'I appreciate this, Gideon. My patient contact is so limited, it's nice to know how my work actually affects people. Thanks.'

'Since this condition is one for the medical journals,

I thought you'd be interested. Maybe you can even publish your findings.' He lifted an eyebrow. 'Now, if you only had an answer for our epidemic. . .'

# CHAPTER EIGHT

NATALIE'S hackles rose. She was in charge of the only microbiology lab in town, and the responsibility to find the cause of the community's malady weighed heavily on her. She knew what was expected of her; she didn't need any reminders.

Motioning to the countertops cluttered with Petri dishes, requisition forms and a multitude of vials and chemical solutions, she said stiffly, 'I'm doing the best I can, Gideon. I'm not a miracle-worker.'

He glanced around the room. 'I see.'

What he saw she didn't know, but one thing was certain—she wouldn't be so forgiving if he questioned her abilities as he had yesterday. She straightened her shoulders, met his gaze straight-on and mentally dared him to continue.

As if he sensed that he was pressing an extremely painful spot, he merely said, 'Let me know—'

'When I find something,' she finished, maintaining her pose. 'Don't worry, you'll be the first to hear.' Along with countless others, she silently added.

With a jaunty salute, he left.

Natalie returned to her workstation and breathed a tired sigh at the task awaiting her.

Over the next few hours, she re-examined her findings in the morgue-like quiet of her lab. Deep in concentration, she pored over piles of notes and sifted through information in her search for any common denominators between the afflicted patients. . .

'Are you still here?' A man's voice came from a distance.

Keeping her attention fixed on her papers, she replied absentmindedly, ''Fraid so.'

A warm hand on her upper spine brought a gasp to her lips and she jumped, twisting to face the unexpected visitor. 'Gideon,' she chided, 'you scared me to death.'

His five-o'clock shadow accentuated the dimple in his cheek. 'Sorry,' he said, unrepentant. He tapped his wristwatch. 'Don't you know what time it is?'

Natalie glanced at the clock on the wall behind him. Eight-thirty—well past the normal end of her shift. 'I didn't notice,' she confessed. 'I'm sure I would have though, when the sun set.'

'It will in about thirty minutes. I suppose you haven't eaten?'

Before she could answer, her stomach growled its assent. 'I heard that,' he told her. 'Let's go.'

'I really shouldn't. . .' she began, even though she suddenly felt ravenous now that food had been mentioned.

'Are you on the verge of a breakthrough?'

'Unfortunately, no.' Sighing, she tossed her pencil on the notepad. 'I feel as if I'm missing a piece, but I don't know what it is.'

'Then you need a break,' he declared. 'One without any shop-talk whatsoever. When you come back, you'll have a fresh perspective.'

'I hope you're right.' She rose to wash her hands. 'Haven't you already had dinner?'

He shook his head. 'Katie went with some friends to the mall and a movie, so I had to fend for myself. Nothing sounded appealing at the time.'

'What brings you here now? A patient?'

Looking sheepish, he replied, 'You seemed a little tense when I left, so I had a feeling you'd stay late.'

'Brilliant deduction,' she replied, flattered by his willingness to seek her out. She grabbed her purse. 'Where shall we go?'

'The cafeteria's oriental buffet is supposed to be good today.'

'Sitr-fry sounds perfect.'

A short time later, Gideon ushered her to a corner table for two with their plates of lo mein, broccoli beef and cashew chicken on rice. Once they were seated, he saturated his food with soy sauce.

She stared, surprised by his action.

'I know, I know,' he said, setting the shaker bottle on the table. 'It's full of sodium. Unfortunately, bland stir-fried food is sacrilegious, and hospitals are notorious for their lack of seasoning. I promise not to eat any salt tomorrow.'

Natalie grinned and let the subject drop. 'What would Katie like for her birthday next month?'

'I had no idea what to get her myself,' he admitted, 'until she mentioned something about displaying our mother's thimble collection. One of my patients is a carpenter, so I bought a case from him.' He wrinkled his face in thought. 'Any handmade craft will thrill her.'

A pattern graph of a quilt draped over an antique rocker came to mind, and she decided to cross-stitch the nostalgic picture as her special gift. Although it would be close, if she worked steadily she should finish it in time. 'Are you planning a big party?'

He shook his head, winding noodles around his fork. 'Her friends invited her out for supper, so we decided to have everyone come to the house afterwards for birthday cake and ice-cream.'

'No low-fat frozen yogurt for diet-conscious swimmers?' Natalie asked, pretending horror. 'Dr Alexander, I'm surprised at you.'

Gideon threw up his hands in a gesture of surrender. 'Katie suggested the menu.'

'In that case, you're forgiven.' She angled her cutlery across the plate and wiped her mouth with a paper napkin.

'Missed a spot,' he said.

She rubbed her lips again.

He shook his head. 'No good. Here, let me.' Taking her napkin, he leaned across the table and dabbed her cheek.

His touch was more of a caress than a brisk let's-wash-it-off action. The left side of her face tingled, as if an electrical current had rushed through.

The urge to grab his hand and hold it against her skin moved upon her like a knee-jerk reflex, but she stifled the impulse. Holding herself still, she submitted to his tender ministrations. What wonderful hands, she thought.

'There.' With a satisfied expression, Gideon settled back into his chair.

The sparks remained, drifting outward from the center of the place he'd stroked high on her face. She brushed her cheekbone, trying unsuccessfully to calm her jangling nerve-endings. His amused expression caught her attention and raised her suspicions.

She narrowed her eyes and spoke. 'I didn't have food on my face. Did I?'

The indentation in his cheek became pronounced. 'Maybe.' One broad shoulder lifted. 'Maybe not.'

'I can see I won't get a straight answer out of you,' she said, enjoying a rare glimpse of his lighthearted side.

'Of course not. Doctors are just like lawyers—we never say what we mean. Besides, you should be grateful I didn't use a desperate mother's technique. I could have wet the tissue with my—'

'I appreciate your thoughtfulness,' she interrupted, returning his smile. His teasing countenance made her wonder what he must have been like during the happier days of his youth.

He stacked the empty plates and trash onto one tray. 'Want a fortune cookie?'

'I didn't see any. Did you?'

'No, but I'll ask.'

He strode across the cafeteria to dispose of the remains, his bearing regal even as he performed such a mundane task. A few steps later his tall frame disappeared into the service area.

Natalie sipped her glass of water, thinking of how enjoyable the past hour had been. She'd eaten the cafeteria's oriental fare before, and judged it palatable, but today she honestly didn't recall tasting the cuisine. She'd been too engrossed in Gideon's company to pay attention to such a minor detail.

The more time she spent with him, the more she craved. Every moment seemed to be a new learning experience as she discovered new facets to his personality. She'd never imagined he'd have a humorous streak, but it was there. Hidden from the most casual observer, perhaps, but none the less it existed. She wondered what other frivolous character traits he might have buried beneath life's huge load of responsibility.

In fact, she hadn't detected any aspect that she considered negative. She loved everything about him because each quality made Gideon Alexander unique.

Natalie's breath caught. She *loved* him. The girl who'd promised to be self-sufficient, independent and wary of medical men had fallen in love with a physician.

Caught up in her thoughts, she didn't notice her uninvited guest until the woman had slid into Gideon's vacant chair.

Kathy Arnold, one of St Mark's respiratory therapists, leaned forward as if imparting a secret. 'You sly thing, you. How did you manage to eat with Dr Gideon?'

'Lucky, I guess.' The less said around Kathy, the better. The woman's attitude toward the opposite sex reminded Natalie of a piranha at feeding-time, and her less than formal reference to the physician hadn't gone unnoticed.

'Isn't Dr Gideon the greatest doctor we've ever gotten?' Kathy gushed. 'And such a heartthrob. Whoever snags him will have to be the best or else they won't keep him, don't you think? Can you see him with someone who's ugly, or dumpy?'

She rattled on, leaving no time for Natalie to reply. 'Of course not. He's the kind who isn't satisfied with anything unless it's perfect. I know. I've worked on a number of his patients.'

Natalie's smile froze on her face. Kathy wasn't known for her tact, but if she'd intended to draw blood with her 'perfect' remarks she had succeeded.

'Oh, I don't know,' Natalie replied airily. 'I'm certain he realizes—as do most people—that no one is *perfect*. Everyone has flaws of one kind or another.'

A pleasant-sounding voice over the intercom system

interrupted. 'Three-four, call twelve.'

Recognizing the summons for the on-duty RT tech to telephone the intensive care unit, Natalie watched Kathy hop out of the chair. 'Gotta go,' the gossipy redhead said, wiggling her fingers in a goodbye wave. 'See ya later.'

Thankful for the interruption, Natalie pushed aside Kathy's comments with a great deal of effort. She refused to dwell on her imperfections—not with her dreaded annual audiology checkup coming up tomorrow.

When Gideon reappeared a few seconds later, she offered him a bright smile. 'Find any?'

He sank into the chair, sending a fresh wave of his woodsy scent in her direction. 'One. We'll have to share.' Breaking the cookie into two equal pieces, he pulled out the scrap of paper caught inside. His face remained impassive as he read it.

'What does it say? The usual stuff about today being your lucky day?'

He grinned. 'Hey, you're pretty sharp. For that, you can have half of it.'

'Half of the cookie or half of the fortune?' she teased.

'You'd better take the part you can eat. Half of a nonexistent fortune is still nothing.'

'Visiting hours are now over,' the female voice intoned over the loudspeaker.

Without waiting for the announcer to finish the standard message, Natalie rose. 'It's late. I'd better go,' she said, feeling like the fabled Cinderella when the clock began to strike twelve. In Natalie's case, she had three hours less to spend with her Prince Charming.

'Home, or back to work?' Gideon asked, accompanying her to the door, his hand hovering at the small of her back.

'Work,' she replied. Fully conscious of his touch, she shivered; with every fiber she wished she could spend a few minutes—or even a lifetime—tucked in his embrace.

'Why don't you get a good night's sleep instead?' he coaxed. 'It might help.'

A vision of a bare-chested Gideon, long legs and tangled sheets rose unbidden. She stumbled over the carpet pattern and quickly pulled herself together—physically and mentally. 'Is that an order, Doctor?'

'Should it be?'

'If it is, I won't follow it,' she warned him.

'What if I make it a request instead?'

Moved by his concern, she stopped. 'Sorry. I've got to have peace and quiet so I can think. It's in short supply during my regular hours.'

'Somehow I knew you wouldn't listen,' he said without rancor.

Companionable silence filled the walk back to the lab. After he'd escorted her to their point of origin, he asked, 'Mind if I stick around for a while?'

'If you'd like.'

Going to the counter with her papers cluttering its surface, she showed him the charts and graphs she'd made. 'I can't seem to find anything connecting these people together. They weren't eating the same foods or doing the same things. No one has gone on any extended trips or been to any exotic places.'

'Have we gotten any viral culture reports yet?'

'Only a preliminary, and it was negative. That doesn't mean something won't show up later, though.'

He rubbed his shadowed jawline, his dark whiskers making a faint rasping sound.

'The only things I haven't spent a lot of time looking for are parasites,' she added.

Gideon paused. 'You've done some O and P studies on my patients, haven't you?'

Natalie nodded. 'A few. They were all negative. If I remember correctly, though, they were done before we recognized a widespread problem.'

'Maybe you should—'

'I think I'll—'

She giggled as they both spoke at once. 'If you're suggesting I start hunting for parasites, we must be thinking on the same wavelength.'

He nodded. 'Might as well be thorough, and rule out everything we can.'

She tapped her cheek, considering which samples she should use. 'I'll begin with the last ones I've received,' she decided.

Natalie rose and retrieved two of the specimens which had arrived during her late meal. After tugging on a pair of protective gloves, she quickly treated portions of each watery stool with a preservative and smeared a minute amount of the thin mixture onto several glass slides.

She stained two of them with iodine and had soon placed them under the teaching microscope with its dual heads. 'Want to see?'

'Sure.' Gideon sat on the countertop's edge to peer into the second set of eyepieces. His familiar earthy scent drifted toward her, and she inhaled deeply as she scanned the slide. Time seemed suspended as she studied each field with painstaking detail.

'Well?' he finally demanded in the silence.

'I don't know. There is something suspicious-looking. . .' Her voice faded away. Clicking on the green lighted pointer, she guided the arrow to the item in question. 'See the small circle?'

'Hmm. What is it?'

'I can't say. It's isn't staining with the iodine, so it could be nothing. It is, however, similar in size and structure to a mature parasite's cyst.' Natalie replaced the slide with another.

A few minutes later she remarked, 'How interesting.'

'What?'

'This person has those same non-staining forms, too.' Tearing her gaze away from her study, she stared into Gideon's eyes. 'I think we've found something significant,' she said.

'The circles?' he guessed.

She nodded, her suspicion growing into certainty. Jumping out of the chair, she hurried to the sink. 'I don't know why I didn't think of it sooner. It's the exact size and shape of cryptosporidium.'

'Are you sure?'

Grabbing the unused slides she'd made earlier, she began dipping them in the various jars of colored liquid. 'I will be in a few minutes. If they show up with this acid-fast technique—which is the same one we use to stain for tuberculosis—then I'm right. If not. . .'

This time, when she sat in front of the microscope, Gideon needed no prompting to look for himself.

With bated breath, she fine-tuned the focus to obtain a clear, sharp image of the field. The sight awaiting her was like finding the pot of gold at the end of the proverbial rainbow.

A glow spread outward and manifested itself in her slow grin. Once again, for Gideon's benefit, she moved the pointer to the structure in question. 'Recognize it?'

'Yes.' Gideon straightened from his cramped position, his eyes mirroring her own excitement. 'You did it, Nat. Congratulations.'

With his hand splayed across her back, her smile widened until her mouth ached. 'You know,' she said, becoming serious, 'I'm really surprised about this. Crypto has always been associated with HIV-positive patients—not the general population.'

'It affects *any* immunocompromised person,' he corrected her. 'Which is probably why children and the elderly were hit the hardest.'

She thought a moment. 'Then how did so many people in town get it? I know the parasite is common in animals—especially cattle—but I doubt if most of the sick people have been around livestock.'

'Don't forget where you live,' Gideon reminded her. 'We're surrounded by feedlots of steers waiting for their turn at the packing plant. Keep in mind, too, that crypto is transmitted through water.'

Understanding dawned. 'Oh!' Natalie exclaimed. 'I'll bet the runoff caused by all of our rain was loaded with the stuff. It seeped into our water supply—'

'Exposing everyone in town,' he finished.

'What about the patients? How will we stop the disease from spreading?' Her eyes grew wide.

'In healthy people, the diarrhea will eventually disappear without any treatment. The others will require supportive care. Until the state epidemiologist tracks down and verifies the cause, the best thing to do is boil all water for consumption. I'm sure someone from the Health Department will issue a Press statement to that effect.'

'But I thought the city treated the water before it was piped into homes.'

'Chlorine doesn't kill this microorganism like it does other bacteria.' He added, 'You'd better notify the county and state medical officials as soon as possible, so they can get their investigation underway.'

'I'll call everyone first thing tomorrow.' Natalie glanced at her wristwatch and gasped. 'Make that today. I didn't realize it was past midnight.'

Gideon rose off his makeshift chair, pulling her up and into his embrace. 'I'm so proud of you,' he said as he hugged her.

Tucked under one of his arms, Natalie rested her head against his cheek. 'Thanks.' She pulled away, but only enough to stare into his face. 'I'm glad you stayed.'

His dark eyes glittered with intent as he lowered his head. She raised her chin, her body quivering with anticipation under his heated gaze.

Her lips met his in a bruising, hungry kiss. Rational thought fled from her mind and she closed her eyes, concentrating only on the information being processed through her remaining physical senses.

The sound of breathing and an occasional hoarse growl of delight drifted to her ears. She sampled his mouth, savoring the exotic flavors of ginger and soy sauce bursting in her tastebuds. His face was rough, almost abrasive, and as skin met skin she found the different texture stimulating.

Gideon's warm body pressed full-length against hers, warming her from head to toe and making her aware of his physical response. His heart thumped under her palm at a fast yet steady beat.

He rubbed her back in a circular motion before his hand crept toward her neckline. Long, lean fingers traced the hollow at her throat before they unbuttoned the top three fastenings of her blouse.

His mouth traveled the same path, exploring and sampling her all the way from the tanned hues at her neck to the creamy whiteness where the sun had never touched.

The sensations his tongue created on her overheated skin sent a moan of pleasure rumbling out of her. He nibbled his way back to her lips, where he once again took demanding possession. She ached with wanting, and the feeling intensified as he pressed her hips against his. With a tightened grip, and one step forward, he backed her against the counter as if intending to crawl inside her.

With her thighs pressed against the dull edge, she snaked an arm over his shoulder and around his neck. One leg caught the edge of a pile of scribbled notes, and it landed on the floor with a thump and a rustle.

Ignoring the sound, she inched her hand up his chest to stroke the soft texture of his shirt, the warm skin above his collar, the rough whiskers along his cheek. If only they were in her apartment. . .

As if the same thought had occurred to him, his ardor slowly but surely cooled. With a last, lingering taste, he murmured against her hair, 'We're in the wrong place. Again, I might add.'

His heavy-lidded gaze made his implication obvious. 'We need to work on that,' she whispered, regret searing her soul.

'We will,' he promised. 'We will.'

For the next few seconds he held her as if she were made of glass, with great care and tenderness.

'I should straighten things up and go home,' she said, making no effort to move out of his arms.

He didn't answer right away. Then he said, 'Alone?'

She tipped her chin to look into his eyes. The desire shining out of them spoke eloquently, and she knew without asking what he wanted to hear. Her breath caught in her throat.

'Yes,' she said, sounding hoarse. 'There are. . .are things. . .I need to tell you before we. . .' She inhaled, unsure of how and where to begin. Revealing her father's identity wouldn't be as difficult as discussing the possibility of her becoming totally deaf. Her gaze fell and she plucked at one of his buttons. 'Except I can't do it. . .right now.'

He ran the back of his hand along her jawline. 'Okay,' he said softly. 'I can wait.' His dimple appeared and his white teeth gleamed. 'Not for long, though.' Reluctance evident, he squeezed her one last time before releasing her.

While Gideon gathered the yellow pages scattered across the floor at their feet Natalie restored order where his hands and mouth had roamed, before retrieving the trash can designated for paper products. While they worked together to straighten the room her tumultuous thoughts were harder to bring under control—the sensations she had experienced were too strong to dismiss so easily.

'Time to call it a day,' he remarked when she flipped the dustcover over the microscope.

'I agree. Although I'm really not tired.'

'Adrenalin. If you don't get some rest you'll be

worthless tomorrow. Maybe you should take the day off?'

Walking out of the lab, she shook her head. 'Dream on. When things settle down, I will.'

Gideon walked her through the dimly lit parking lot to her car. 'Get some rest,' he advised.

'I'll try. You do the same.'

His farewell kiss was more of a light caress, but it served to recall her previous experience with vivid detail.

At home, Natalie tried to keep her promise. But sleep wouldn't come.

With wide-awake eyes, she watched the brightness of the morning star dim as the sun's first rays grew stronger and stronger. Anxious to alert the necessary people about her discovery, she hurried back to the hospital feeling as if she'd never left.

Amanda Evans, County Public Health Nurse, was thrilled with Natalie's news, although she'd never heard of the parasite before. The state epidemiologist was excited as well, promising to send someone within hours to investigate.

Karen beamed with pride. 'I knew you'd figure it out,' she told Natalie. 'If this doesn't impress our administrators, I don't know what will.'

'Time will tell,' Natalie replied.

Karen insisted on keeping abreast of current developments, and left the radio blaring. By ten o'clock the announcer had broadcast a 'boil water' advisory from the city's sanitation engineer.

Natalie spent the day accepting congratulations from well-wishing hospital personnel and doctors, as well as fielding requests for information from members of the

Press and the local television studio.

'Thank goodness I have an appointment in thirty minutes,' she announced, after a phone call from a persistent reporter.

'Don't come back until tomorrow, either,' Karen instructed. 'I'll handle the rest. Wasn't it nice of Jim to assign a temporary tech to help us? Now that we have a celebrity in our midst, things around here are going to change.'

'I hope so,' Natalie remarked. 'Unfortunately, this story will be replaced by something else in a few days, and we'll fade back into obscurity.'

Yet, as she drove to her audiology appointment she hoped that her discovery would wake up the right people, making them more willing to fund the improvements she wanted.

It was also clear that secrets had no place in her relationship with Gideon; she had to divulge her father's identity at the earliest opportunity. By the time she arrived at her destination she'd rehearsed her little speech to perfection.

Rob Martin, the young audiologist who had taken over from his father upon his retirement, greeted her as she walked into his office. 'After you being in the news today, I expected you to cancel,' he told her as he led her into the special room for hearing tests.

'Sorry.' Natalie grinned. 'I had to get away. I was tired of answering the same questions over and over.'

'I understand,' he sympathized. Passing the earphones to her, he said, 'You know the routine. Shall we see how you're doing?'

Natalie did indeed know the routine. She climbed into the soundproof box, made herself comfortable and signaled each of the various tones she heard by raising one hand.

The end of the test came quickly, much sooner than she thought usual—especially since she hadn't acknowledged very many sounds.

Worry slowly replaced her uplifted spirits. As she exited the booth Rob's usually cheerful face remained inscrutable, making her stomach tighten into a hard, nauseating knot. Although she wanted to walk out the door and pretend nothing was wrong, she couldn't. The direction of her life hinged on his assessment.

Swallowing the lump of fear in her throat, she asked in a hoarse voice, 'What's the verdict?'

# CHAPTER NINE

Rob crossed his arms. 'There isn't a big change,' he began.

'But there is one,' Natalie stated, focusing on his hazel eyes. 'How bad?'

He frowned, as if uncertain. 'Now, don't think the worst. It's small.'

'How much is small?'

'You've had an extremely stressful day. Tiredness can affect—'

She waved her hands to brush aside his excuses. 'How much?' she repeated.

'Your range of hearing appears to be getting narrower at both the upper and lower ends of the scale. If we repeat it when you're well-rested, we might not see any difference from the previous test.'

'Your dad said the same thing last year,' she told him. 'Small losses eventually add up to big ones.'

'Let's not think the worst,' Rob insisted. 'At some point we may see it stabilize.'

'When?'

'You know I can't predict that,' he chided gently.

Natalie sighed. 'I know.'

'In the meantime, don't anticipate problems. We're seeing advances all the time.' He laid a hand on her shoulder. 'Don't request your hearing ear dog, yet. Okay?'

She forced a smile. He had meant well with his teasing remark. 'Okay,' she murmured.

\*   \*   \*

For the next few hours the swim team required her attention for the most part, and she managed to tamp down the small shafts of fear that sprouted as quickly as buds on yeast.

There were only two times when the dark cloud of despair threatened to overtake her—when her students' encouragement to a six-year-old beginner paddling across the full length of the pool rang in her ears and when the water gently lapped against the sides after the kids had climbed out.

It wasn't until later, when she was alone in her house with no other distractions, that her worries returned with a vengeance.

Throughout the entire evening, while she stitched Katie's birthday picture with misty eyes, her elation at her professional success didn't return to its pre-appointment heights. The thought of living in a world of silence—never to hear the birds chirp, a baby's cry or a loved one's voice—was almost more than she could bear.

Natalie swallowed the burning lump in her throat and ripped out the threads she'd placed in the wrong holes of her cloth. Although Gideon knew of her impairment and still was attracted to her, she questioned whether or not he'd feel the same if she became totally deaf. She didn't know which would be harder to endure—losing her hearing or losing Gideon.

She sighed, forcing herself to quit indulging in self-pity. Life had seemed so simple before she'd fallen in love. . .

Life had been so much simpler in medical school, Gideon thought as he relaxed in his easy chair and paid little attention to the blaring television. His whole being had been focused on textbooks, patients and the hospital; his mother and Katie had come next. Everything else had been incidental.

Although he still had his work and his sister to claim the bulk of his attention, Natalie had become equally important.

'Oh, look!' Katie exclaimed, coming to attention on the sofa. 'Natalie's on the news.'

Gideon pulled himself out of his musing to watch the sixty-second segment. The camera showed a view of Natalie in the small microbiology lab as she talked specifically about her role in the discovery and about laboratory medicine in general.

He wondered if the Denver networks had picked up her story. Harrison Pike would hear of his daughter's success and undoubtedly be proud enough to pop the buttons off his tailored shirt.

When the television anchorman moved to his next topic, Katie remarked in awe, 'Wow. Isn't she the greatest?' Without waiting for her brother's reply, she continued, 'She looks happier on TV than she did this evening at practice.'

'Oh?'

Katie nodded. 'Yeah, she acted like she had something on her mind. I wonder what it was?'

Gideon wondered as well. Rubbing his chin while frowning, he contemplated his next move. Natalie didn't need his help any more—if she'd ever needed it at all. Credited with discovering the cause of the Rocky Hills epidemic, she'd be able to do anything she wanted. As for her department funding, the administrative officers were certain to reconsider their decision; St Mark's couldn't afford to lose her.

He didn't want to lose his time with her either. In fact, he'd prefer to spend more, beginning with right now—this very evening.

Recalling the way she'd felt in his arms, he relaxed his mouth into a small smile. It seemed much longer ago than yesterday—or rather, very early this morning. It took very little effort to conjure up his mental picture of her full lips, her tanned skin and her eyes begging for more of his touch. Even now he could smell the berry fragrance he always associated with her.

His memories dissolved as Katie yawned. 'I'm going to bed. G'night, Gideon.' She disappeared into her room.

He clicked off the set with the remote control and welcomed the silence. Steepling his fingers, he stared at a half-finished crossword puzzle with unseeing eyes, his mind jumping back to the place it had been before Katie had interrupted. He'd wanted to do more, much more, than just kiss Natalie, and she obviously had too.

Physical desire rose, begging for appeasement, and he fidgeted in his chair to lessen the ache. Being a mentor, a guardian angel and a platonic friend wasn't enough any more.

Unfortunately, his pact with her father posed a problem. Having secrets while enjoying an intimate relationship wasn't right. He could spill his guts, and risk Harrison's ability to make good on his threat, but by his doing so Natalie would be devastated.

If she knew her father's arm of influence extended this far, she might never speak to him again—and Gideon couldn't be a party to that. Losing his father at an early age and his mother so recently had taught him to cherish family moments. He couldn't take them from someone he loved.

He sighed. In spite of his altruistic intentions, his desire for honesty remained strong. What he needed was a way to explain the situation so that she wouldn't reject both him and her father.

When he figured out how to accomplish his objective, he'd tell her.

'I heard the news last night, but it was late so I didn't telephone,' Harrison Pike told his daughter the next afternoon. 'It was in this morning's paper as well. Your mother and I are so proud of you.'

'Thanks, Dad,' Natalie replied, feeling her smile stretch from ear to ear and forgetting her tiredness. Although she'd planned to get a good night's rest, to make up for the one before, her tumultuous thoughts hadn't quieted. She'd spent most of the night stitching, stopping only when her eyes had crossed after she'd made hundreds of tiny 'x's.

'I knew you were capable of great things,' he boasted. 'This just proves it. I suppose you did it all on your own?'

'In a way,' she replied. 'Gideon was with me at the time, and we were discussing several possibilities when we both decided to start looking for parasites. Lo and behold, I found them.'

'Gideon?'

Natalie twisted the phone cord. 'Gideon Alexander. He's our newest physician. An internist.'

'Must be a good man.'

'He's wonderful, Dad. You'll have to meet him.'

'Next time we're in town,' he promised, before ending the conversation.

Basking in the glow of her father's praise, Natalie

sailed through the morning—especially when Gideon called.

'I'm sending a twenty-year-old, James Davies, over for a mono-test and a strep titer,' he informed her. 'After being sick at college for about ten days, he's come home.'

'Has he had any antibiotics?'

'The campus doctor gave him penicillin for a strep throat, but Davies says it isn't any better. With his fever and swollen lymph nodes, it's probably a case of infectious mononucleosis.'

'I'll have the results in about forty-five minutes,' Natalie promised.

'I wanted a culture, too, but he left before Becky could swab his throat. Can you—?'

'No problem,' she answered.

'Afterwards send him home,' Gideon ordered. 'I'll call him as soon as I have the results.'

Ten minutes later she was notified that the patient in question had arrived. After the phlebotomist had drawn his blood sample, she took a tongue depressor and said, 'Open wide.' While he gagged, exposing the back of his throat, she quickly swiped the area with a sterile swab.

'All done,' she told him.

'Great,' James replied, his face drawn.

'Are any of your friends sick?' she asked.

He thought a minute. 'Some had the flu, but nothing like this. I sure hope Dr Alexander isn't right about it being mono. I can't afford to lose this semester.'

Privately concurring with Gideon's diagnosis, she said, 'Dr Alexander will have our results in a little while and then he'll call you. Go home and take things easy.'

'I can't do much else,' he complained as he left.

Giving his sample STAT priority, she soon had an answer. 'You were right,' she reported to Gideon over the phone. 'James Davies' mono test is positive.'

'Thanks. I owe you one. Any plans for this evening?'

'Not really.' She stifled a yawn.

'Good. I'll see you tonight.'

She'd barely had time to replace the receiver when the telephone rang again.

'Ms Canfield? I'm Max Nelson, and I'm calling as a representative of the University of Colorado Medical School's Endowment Foundation. I thought you'd be pleased to know our committee has agreed to your proposal and a check will be issued to you in a few weeks.'

'A check? My proposal?' she asked, puzzled.

'Gideon asked us to consider your request for equipment about a week ago. We reviewed the documentation and the foundation would like to support your endeavors,' Max told her. 'You'll receive a formal letter giving more details—'

'Wait,' she interrupted. '*Gideon* did this?'

Max chuckled. 'He didn't tell you? He's good about taking charge.'

'He certainly is,' she agreed, uncertain if she should be thrilled or irritated at Gideon's clandestine actions.

'We went to medical school together.'

'You did?' Momentarily shelving her blossoming annoyance, she seized the opportunity to gain some answers to her long-held questions. 'Didn't you want a rural practice like Gideon?'

Max laughed. 'I'm a city boy, through and through.'

'We're lucky to get Gideon,' she began, her heart

thumping with anticipation. 'He almost moved to Benchwood Springs instead.'

Max became serious. 'Yeah. We were surprised when he changed his mind at the last minute. No one knew or understood why. He wouldn't discuss it either.'

Her spirits dropped. Another dead end. Trying to hide her disappointment, she said brightly, 'Their loss is our gain.'

'Actually, it's *your* gain,' he emphasized. 'If it hadn't been for Gideon, your request would never have been considered. You're very fortunate.'

She wouldn't have been more shocked if he'd dumped a bucket of icy water over her head.

'I guess I am,' she ground out.

'By the way, congratulations are also in order for identifying the source of your outbreak. I'm not surprised—Gideon spoke highly of you.'

'Oh, he did?' Natalie couldn't wait to talk to Gideon this evening. She'd planned to discuss her worsening impairment, in addition to her father, but now she added this recent development to her mental agenda.

'Yeah. Anyway, good luck with your work.'

The conversation ended and she carefully replaced the receiver. Tugging on a lock of hair, she bit her lower lip.

'Bad news?' Karen asked as she walked in the room.

Natalie shrugged and forced a small semblance of a smile to her mouth. 'No—why?'

'You normally don't frown.'

'Well, everything's fine.' Natalie didn't want to discuss Max's announcement until she'd straightened out a few things with Gideon first. She slipped out of her lab coat and hung it over a chair. 'I'll leave everything in your capable hands. See you tomorrow.'

While driving home Max's comments continued to sting. 'If it hadn't been for Gideon, your request would never have been considered.'

Gideon had to have pulled some influential strings. Why else would Max have worded his remark as he had?

Her ire built with each passing block. Gideon knew how much she wanted to succeed on her own. He couldn't, *wouldn't* have done something so underhanded, part of her insisted. Yet the facts were undeniable.

Maybe he simply forgot to tell you? her inner voice defended. Things have been rather hectic lately.

That had to be it, she decided, clutching to the idea like a man hanging onto a liferaft. Gideon was too trustworthy to encourage her to proceed on her own and then take matters into his own hands. She might not be the world's best judge of character—Mason Campbell came to mind—but her intuition said that Gideon was a man of integrity.

No, she couldn't—shouldn't—jump to conclusions. Loving someone meant trusting them, and Gideon, being the man she loved, deserved her loyalty. Comfortable with her decision, she parked in a car stall outside the apartment complex.

As she reached for the door handle another thought clicked into place. She jerked her head up to stare straight ahead through the windshield, her breath coming out in a huge gasp.

Her father, Harrison Pike, served on the university's Endowment Foundation board of directors; the same organization sending her money.

Don't jump to conclusions, she reminded herself.

There has to be a perfectly logical explanation.

Gideon couldn't have been in cahoots with Harrison—he'd admitted he'd only met her father on one occasion. He wouldn't lie to her about something so important.

Would he?

Gideon bounded through the apartment complex and came to an abrupt stop outside the door labeled 3B. It was strange how he could detect traces of her special fragrance the moment he entered the building, considering the number of people who lived there. 'Natalie,' he shouted as he pressed the bell. 'Open up.'

Hearing nothing, he pounded with a closed fist, unwilling to give up. He *had* to talk to her. Ever since Max had called him with the good news, he'd been worried about Natalie's reaction. He should have told her what he'd done—he'd planned to, in fact—but it had slipped his mind.

He pounded again, this time rattling the knob at the same time. The door swung wide, revealing her tidy living-room. 'Natalie?' he called, stepping over the threshold into the homey inviting atmosphere within.

The aquarium gurgled a reply. 'Natalie?' he called again, crossing the room in three long strides to peek into the kitchen. It was empty.

Backtracking, he considered her habit of solitary walks but swiftly dismissed the idea. She wouldn't have wandered far, knowing that he was coming.

Her bedroom door stood slightly ajar, and he stuck his head through the opening. A figure lay on the bed, curled into a ball and facing the wall.

His shoulders slumped with relief as he let out a long breath. He advanced to the opposite side of the bed, his footsteps muffled by the carpeting. Seeing her wrinkled forehead, he carefully lowered himself onto the mattress to stretch out beside her. Resting on one elbow, he brushed aside an errant curl before smoothing away the lines between her eyebrows.

Katie had mentioned Natalie's preoccupation last night. Although Natalie had sounded okay when he'd talked to her today, she'd obviously hidden whatever was bothering her. Whatever it was must be serious if she couldn't relax even when asleep.

Leaning closer, he brushed a light kiss on her forehead before moving to her mouth. Rewarded by a drowsy smile, he lay back and pulled her into his embrace with the same care he'd given to newborns during med school. He tucked her under his arm, her head fitting in the crook of his shoulder, and nuzzled her hair, inhaling her light scent.

'Wake up, Sleeping Beauty,' he murmured, stroking her bared arms and luxuriating in her softness.

'Gideon,' she murmured, nestling into his warmth. 'How did you get in?'

'Through the door. Unlocked, I might add. Rocky Hills may be a small town but leaving—' An elbow in his chest stopped his sentence.

Natalie sat upright. 'How did you get in?' she asked, frowning.

'Through the door,' he repeated, surprised by her agitation.

A look of horror appeared, and she covered her ears. 'Oh, my God.'

'What's wrong?' he asked, pulling himself into a sitting position and grabbing her arm. 'What's wrong?' he repeated as she removed then re-inserted her hearing-aids.

She stared at him, disbelief etching her features. 'I can't hear you,' she said brokenly.

*I can't hear.* The words echoed in her mind as she studied the floor. Her world of silence was supposed to come gradually, not descend all at once. *I can't hear.* She felt her mouth move, and knew she had spoken the words.

Gideon tilted her chin upward, causing her to look directly at his face. His mouth moved. 'Just relax. Tell me what I can do.'

She shook her head, closing her eyes to keep the tears at bay.

He gripped her upper arms and gave her a slight shake. Her lids flew open and she fixed Gideon in her sights.

'Battery?' he mouthed, his eyebrows drawn into a line and his eyes dark with intent.

Of course. She hadn't thought of that. Nodding, she removed the aids. Gideon released his hold and she bounded off the bed to yank on a dresser drawer. Bringing out a small package, she returned to the bed and sat next to him while she replaced the tiny power packs. With bated breath, she placed the mechanism in her ears and waited.

'Is that better?' he asked.

She froze at the sound of his voice, relief making her slump against him.

Strong arms encircled her. 'Natalie? Can you hear me?' His tone was insistent and worried.

She nodded, meeting his dark-eyed gaze. 'Yes. Oh, Gideon, yes, I can.'

His face relaxed. In the next instant she found herself flat on her back with her arms around his neck. He hovered above her, resting on his elbows. 'Hasn't this ever happened before?' he demanded.

'No. I've always replaced the batteries on a regular basis, but I've had a lot on my mind lately and I obviously forgot.' She felt her face warm. 'I went a little crazy, didn't I? Sorry.'

'Don't be,' he said, looking down on her with tenderness. 'But I can't imagine you reacting so strongly without reason. What *has* been on your mind?'

Pinned underneath him, she was aware of his masculine scent mingled with the freshness of her sheets. She fingered a button on his shirt and chewed on her lower lip. This was an opening, and although she wanted to avoid the subject, she couldn't.

'I had my annual hearing checkup yesterday. It wasn't good.' Her chin quivered and she blinked.

'How much worse?'

She cleared her throat and swallowed. 'Not much, but if I continue losing ground I'll eventually become totally deaf.' Delivering her words in a flat tone, she stared at the hollow in his throat.

'No wonder you were so worried just now.' Gideon shifted his weight, freeing one hand to cup the right side of her face. She raised her gaze to meet his brown one. 'Did you think it would matter to me?'

She nodded, her attention fixed. Loving concern— not revulsion—shone out of his face.

'It doesn't,' he reassured her, stroking her cheek with his thumb. 'I love you, regardless.'

'You do?'

Crows' feet appeared around his eyes, and his mouth curved into a gentle smile, revealing straight teeth and his endearing dimple. 'Yeah, I do.'

'I love you, too,' she whispered, her heart pounding

in an accelerated steady rhythm. There was nothing she wanted more than what was inevitable.

Gideon's mouth moved upon hers, and she returned his kiss with all her might. His hands roamed across her body in a searching pattern. Raising the hem of her cotton T-shirt, he slid his fingers across the smooth, warm flesh.

He paused from his onslaught to murmur against her cheek. 'At least we're in the right place.'

'About. . .time,' she murmured in breathy snatches.

'Impatient, were we?'

'Were we?' she returned.

'Definitely,' he replied, nuzzling her neck.

'Then what are we waiting for?'

'Not a thing.' Under his skilful hands she felt her body temperature rise and an ache build in the very center of her being.

He raised her arms, releasing her mouth only long enough to whip off her shirt. The cool air brought goosebumps to her bared skin and she struggled with his buttons, fighting to free him from his clothing. Frustrated by her lack of success, and eager for his warmth, she yanked on the shirt placket and popped off the last uncooperative button.

Gideon twisted onto his side, bringing Natalie with him. Hands fumbled at waistbands, the scratchy sound of metal teeth harsh in the silence.

'I should warn you,' she breathed against his ear, 'I'm not—'

'Not to worry. I'll—'

The telephone jangled and he stiffened.

'They can. . .leave a. . .message,' Natalie murmured.

It rang three times before the answering machine

whirred to record the caller. Katie's impatient voice filled the air. 'Natalie? I'm looking for Gideon. If you know where—'

He rolled across the bed to yank the receiver off its cradle. 'Yeah, I'm here.'

Natalie waited with bated breath, concerned over the girl's agitation.

'We were in the middle of something.' He winked and leaned over to caress her bare shoulder. 'What's up?' He paused. 'Okay, I'll be there in a few minutes.' He hung up.

'The hospital?' she guessed.

He shook his head and looked apologetic. 'There's a delivery man at our house with a letter. He won't let Katie sign for it—says he has to put it directly in my hands.' He scooted closer and hugged her. 'I'm sorry.'

She grinned. 'Don't be. It isn't your fault. One of these days we won't be interrupted.'

'Yeah. On our honeymoon.' He grinned.

'Oh, Gideon,' she murmured, both stunned and thrilled at the prospect.

Gideon's dark eyes twinkled. 'Is that a yes or a no?'

Natalie wiggled against him. 'A definite yes.' She became apologetic. 'But I'm not good at socializing. Doctors' wives should be. My deafness could also be a hindrance.'

'Who says?' he countered, running a finger along her lower jawline.

'Our children may have a tendency toward hearing problems,' she warned him.

'Then you'll teach us sign language. Now, stop worrying.'

Suddenly she pulled a few inches away. If Gideon

was to become a member of her family he had to know about her father—and preferably before they were introduced. 'I have to tell you something else,' she began. 'My father is Harrison Pike, the orthopedic surgeon.'

His eyes lost their sparkle and became intense. 'So?'

She shrugged, surprised yet pleased by his indifference.

His dimple returned. 'Don't worry. I won't ask for any special favors—except to take his daughter off his hands.'

Playfully swatting him, she said, 'Gee, thanks.'

'Get dressed,' he ordered, swinging his legs off the bed to stand. 'You're coming with me.'

Arriving at his house, she noticed the dark blue sedan parked curbside. 'I hope it's not bad news,' she replied, watching Gideon for a reaction.

He shrugged. 'We'll find out soon enough.' Escorting her inside with his hand hovering on her spine, he entered the living-room to find a middle-aged man dressed in a crisp brown suit sipping coffee with Katie.

After placing his mug on the end table, the stranger rose. 'Dr Gideon Alexander?'

'Yes,' Gideon replied.

The man handed him a white business envelope. 'Pleased to meet you. I'm sorry I couldn't give this to your sister. I had orders to hand it directly to you.' He turned to Katie. 'Thank you for your hospitality. I'll be on my way.'

He closed the door behind him, a quiet click marking his exit. Natalie and Katie stared at Gideon as he tapped the sealed correspondence against an open palm. His expression was fearsome, reminding Natalie of how he'd looked when she'd met him for the first time.

'Aren't you going to open it?' Katie's eyes were wide.

Gideon's mouth formed a hard line.

Natalie laid a hand on his arm. 'Gideon, what's wrong? You need to open it. It must be something important.'

Katie strode closer. 'Oh, for heaven's sakes. If you won't open it,' she said, exasperated, 'I will.' With that, she ripped it out of his hand and turned her back to him.

'Katie,' he bellowed, reaching around her to take possession.

Katie rested her hands on her hips and glared at him. 'I wasn't going to open it.' Her tone became questioning. 'Whoever lives on Cedar Park Drive must want you to, though. They sure went to a lot of trouble for some crummy letter.'

'Cedar Park Drive?' Natalie echoed, her stomach churning with a fresh surge of acid.

'Do you recognize the street?' Katie asked, intent on solving the mystery.

Natalie stared at Gideon, her gaze as cold as ice. 'I lived there.' She paused. 'Didn't I?'

Gideon rubbed his face. 'Look, I can explain—'

'I'll bet you can,' Natalie ground out. 'No wonder you didn't seem surprised when I told you about my father. You already knew. Didn't you?'

# CHAPTER TEN

NATALIE'S voice rose. 'Didn't you?'

Gideon's eyes turned bleak and he nodded, almost imperceptibly.

She wiped her cold sweaty palms on her thighs, dug her hands into her denim pockets and backed away. 'How long have you known?'

'Since April.'

The loose ends finally came together. 'My father sent you here. That's why you didn't go to Benchwood Springs,' she remarked in amazement. Her tone hardened. 'What did he bribe you with?'

'What's going on?' Katie asked, her head bobbing back and forth between Natalie and Gideon.

'Later,' they responded in unison.

Gideon advanced. 'It wasn't a bribe.'

Natalie tossed her head. 'Yeah, right.'

'It wasn't,' he insisted. 'It was more like—' he paused '—coercion.'

Tears burned in her eyes. 'You've manipulated me from the very beginning.' Another issue came to the fore. 'Was the foundation thing his idea, too?'

'No.' He was adamant. 'It was mine.'

'I'm surprised. My father serves on the board, and has for as long as I can remember.'

Gideon blinked and slowly shook his head from side to side. 'I didn't realize.' He tossed the envelope onto a chair, took two steps toward her and clasped her shoulders. 'I know what you're thinking, but you're wrong. Everything you've accomplished, you've done yourself.'

'Have I?' she asked, the taste of betrayal bitter in her mouth.

'Yes. The grant money, solving our epidemic—everything. It happened because of *you*.'

'That's not how your friend Max tells the story.'

Gideon's eyes narrowed. 'What did he say?'

The unspoken words burned in her throat and she couldn't force them past her lips.

His grip tightened. 'What did he say?' he repeated through clenched teeth.

'"If it hadn't been for Gideon, your request would never have been considered." That's a direct quote,' she said flatly.

'I didn't pull any strings, Nat. I told you a long time ago that I wouldn't interfere, and I didn't. As for my coming to Rocky Hills, your father wanted me here to give you moral support—that's all.'

'Protect me, you mean.'

Gideon flared. 'What's wrong with that? Everyone could use a helping hand now and then.'

'How noble. Should I call you St Gideon?' Sarcasm laced her words.

His face resembled a thundercloud.

'Go ahead—open the letter. I'm sure your payment's inside, along with further instructions.'

'Natalie,' he warned her through clenched teeth.

'What else did you lie about?'

He gripped her shoulders. 'I didn't lie, but I couldn't say anything either. I had orders to keep our alliance confidential.'

'Pardon me,' she said, without meaning it. 'What else did you *neglect* to tell me?'

'That's it. There's nothing else.'

'What about the other things you told me?'

'All true. I love you.'

'Trust and love go together, Gideon,' she reminded him. Tears came to her eyes and she stared at the ceiling to keep them from spilling down her face. 'When Max first gave me the news I thought you'd gone against your word, but something wouldn't let me believe it. Then, even after I realized my father could have been involved, I still told myself that you were worthy of my trust—that you wouldn't betray me.'

'I didn't.'

She focused on his face, on his worried eyes in particular. The sincerity she saw conflicted with her own perception of the situation, and she felt as if she'd been sucked into a vortex. She didn't know what to think anymore; nothing was as it had seemed or as she'd expected.

Suddenly she rubbed her temples in a circular motion. 'I need to go.'

'I'll take you home.'

Natalie shook her head and wrenched out of his grasp. 'No.' She addressed Katie. 'Can you drive?'

'Yes, but I don't think—' the teen spluttered.

'Then let's go.' Natalie strode toward the door.

Katie hesitated. Staring at her brother with wide, troubled eyes, she asked in a tentative voice, 'Gideon?'

He kneaded the back of his neck. 'Take her home,' he said wearily.

Katie drove across town without the radio blaring, as was her usual custom. On this occasion Natalie would have welcomed the diversion. She stared straight ahead, fists clenched in her lap.

Halfway there, Katie broke the silence. 'He loves you, you know.'

Natalie drew a deep breath and took a few seconds to reply. 'Maybe.'

'He does,' the girl insisted. 'I can tell. Was it really so bad that Gideon kept what he knew a secret?'

Natalie tugged on her hair. 'I don't know.'

Katie persisted. 'Or are you just mad at your dad and taking it out on Gideon?'

Natalie looked at her. 'For sixteen, you're very perceptive. At this point I don't know what I feel. Hurt, mostly. I just can't believe my father had the nerve to send someone to watch over me.'

'Parents do strange things sometimes. Mom always said there were things I wouldn't understand until I was one.' She stopped the car near the front entrance. 'Please give Gideon and your dad another chance.'

The tears in Katie's eyes brought fresh ones to Natalie's, and she offered a weak smile. 'I don't know if I can.'

'You have to try. Gideon and I need you. Won't you let him explain his side of things?' Katie pleaded.

'We'll see.'

Katie's comments echoed in Natalie's mind throughout the evening, but the sense of betrayal wouldn't leave. Somehow, because she loved him, Gideon's actions hurt far worse. He might not have known at first how badly she wanted to be away from her father's influence, but later he had. Why hadn't he righted the wrong then? Why had he continued the deception?

Gideon held the fateful envelope in his hand before savagely ripping it open. He scanned the pages in disbelief—Harrison Pike had enclosed the original letter of recommendation. The same one promised upon the end of his contract. A reward for a job well done.

His victory, if it could be called one, seemed hollow. He'd regained control of his future, but he'd lost something that meant as much to him if not more. Natalie.

The back door slammed and Katie walked into the living-room. 'How was she?' he asked when she sat on the arm of his recliner.

'Upset. I tried to talk to her. You hurt her, Gideon. You and her nutty father. Why didn't he just leave her alone?' she demanded, pouting.

Gideon sighed. 'He wanted to protect her, and in the process I ended up in the middle.'

'How did it happen?'

'Dr Pike sent for me one day and suggested that I move to Rocky Hills to keep an eye on Natalie. If I refused, he said he'd ruin my chances to get accepted into an infectious disease program.' He shrugged. 'Spending a few years in this community seemed a small price to pay to guarantee my future so I agreed, never dreaming I'd fall in love with her. I would have told her—risked my future—but the news would have ruined her relationship with her family, so I kept quiet.'

Katie hugged him. 'Tell her. She'll understand.'

'I hope so,' he said fervently. 'I certainly hope so.'

Natalie's phone call to her father was short and not so sweet. 'I know what you've done,' she told Harrison, without any preamble. 'You promised not to interfere in my life after the last time.'

Harrison remained silent, and she pictured her father's familiar pensive expression.

'How did you force Gideon into coming here when he had other plans?'

His tired voice came over the wire. 'In exchange for helping you, I said I'd see that he was able to pursue his specialty. If he didn't. . .' The statement went unfinished.

'Oh, Dad,' Natalie moaned, knowing how much Gideon's goal meant to him. Her chin dropped in her chest as she covered her eyes with her free hand. 'Why?'

'Your mother and I only wanted to protect you.'

'But you promised you'd let me manage on my own. No one was supposed to give me any special favors.'

He paused. 'What are you going to do?'

'I'm not sure,' she answered, knowing that he was really asking if she planned to relocate. Again.

She didn't really want to start over, yet how could she ever face Gideon again?

'Some of the nurses are throwing a party,' Karen mentioned ten days later. 'Mrs Patterson has finally been discharged after her surgery. The way it sounds, no one was sad to see her go.'

'Hmm,' Natalie replied absentmindedly.

'By the way, Mrs Paxton—the lady with the fungal infection in her sinuses—didn't make it. Becky asked me to tell you since Dr Alexander couldn't reach you.'

The news caught Natalie's attention. Her memory of the case was bittersweet, since Gideon had worked so closely with her on it.

'When *are* you going to talk to him? The poor man's been leaving messages for over a week,' Karen scolded. 'I'm getting to the point where I hate to answer the phone.'

Natalie tossed an outdated box of culture plates into

the trash and reached into the refrigerator for another. 'I don't know.'

'You've withdrawn from everyone, you know.'

'Sorry,' she said, unrepentant.

'You can't hide forever.'

Natalie shrugged. 'I'm not hiding.'

'You're not?' Karen glanced at the clock. 'Gee, I thought you were supposed to leave hours ago and you're still here.'

'I'm catching up on my work.'

'Cleaning out refrigerators isn't a top priority item. It's one of those things people tackle only when they're desperate for something to do. Go talk to Gideon.'

'I can't.'

'Why not?' Karen stared over her reading glasses with narrowed eyes.

'First of all, I'm embarrassed. How would you react if your father had blackmailed someone you loved?'

'You're not responsible for your father's actions,' Karen reminded her.

'Maybe not, but I can't help how I feel.'

'That's not the only reason you won't talk to Gideon, is it?'

Natalie shook her head. 'I wonder if he's ever told me the truth. I mean, he said he loved me, but how do I know it wasn't part of the overall plan to soften me up in order to meet my father's terms? Let's get real. If I hated the man, I certainly wouldn't go to him for advice.'

'Do you honestly believe he faked his affection?'

A memory of the intense interlude in Natalie's bedroom returned in vivid detail. She'd almost given him something very precious—something he might not have deserved. Chilled by the idea, she rubbed her arms. 'It's possible,' she maintained.

Karen removed her glasses and wiped the lenses with a tissue. 'How long have we worked together?'

'Over two years,' Natalie supplied. 'So?'

Karen nodded. 'Uh-huh. And in all those months you've never said a word to me about your famous father. If I follow your logic, I could wonder if you've ever told *me* the truth.'

'That's different,' Natalie said flatly.

'How?'

'It just is.'

'Because you love him?'

'Yes. Love and trust go together.' The words gave her a sense of *déjà vu*.

'Along with understanding and forgiveness.'

Another box thumped against the inside of a metal trash can. 'Okay, okay. You've made your point. I'll talk to him.'

'Good.' Karen sounded satisfied. 'If it's any consolation, I hear he's been a real grouch to work with. The sooner you two get back together, the better.' She grinned. 'In fact, why don't you do it now, while your courage is up?'

Natalie fiddled with a lock of hair. 'I don't know where to find him.'

'He was paged a few minutes ago. He's probably still in the hospital.'

'Maybe I should wait,' she mused aloud.

Karen shook her head. 'He's already made the first move. Now it's your turn. The switchboard will know where he is.'

Natalie closed the refrigerator door. Summoning her nerve, she picked up the telephone receiver and soon had a fix on his location. 'He's in Emergency.'

Suddenly, Phil appeared in the doorway. 'Have you heard? Dr Alexander's sister was in a car wreck. She's in pretty bad shape.'

Natalie gasped and she covered her mouth. Shoving the startled tech out of the way, she darted from the room to sprint through the corridors. Let her be okay, was her silent prayer.

Bursting through the ER doors, she stopped at the nurses' desk. 'Where's Katie?'

'Am I glad you're here,' the nurse announced. 'Katie's asking for you. She's in room one.'

'How is she?'

'A few cracked ribs and lacerations. Her leg's the worst—compound fracture of the right femur. Several pieces are shattered.'

Natalie ran into the cubicle and saw Gideon and the ER physician, along with several nurses, clustered around the blood-spattered gurney. She immediately went to Katie's head and stroked her forehead while trying to keep her tears at bay. 'Hi, Katie.'

'Natalie. You came,' the girl replied weakly.

'You bet.' Her voice choked. 'I won't leave you.'

Katie licked her lips. 'Thanks. How bad is it?'

Natalie stole a look at Katie's mangled leg and felt bile rise in her throat. She lifted her gaze to Gideon, and the worry residing in his eyes spoke more eloquently than words.

'Not good,' she told her.

'Where's the orthopedist?' Gideon demanded of no one in particular.

Another nurse hurried in. 'Dr Sullivan was out of town today. I just called his house but he's not back yet.'

Gideon swore.

'We have to amputate,' Dr Thomas, the white-haired ER physician stated.

Natalie gasped.

Katie whimpered.

Gideon stared at the other physician, his expression impassive.

'It has to come off, son,' Dr Thomas repeated. 'We can't repair the damage.'

'No!' Katie and Natalie cried together.

'No,' Natalie repeated, her voice firm. Five pairs of eyes rested on her. 'No,' she insisted a third time. 'Airlift her to Denver. There are good orthopedic surgeons there. They'll be able to do more than you can here.'

Dr Thomas was dubious. 'Maybe, but—'

'Dr Pike can save her leg,' she said. 'He's very good with bone reconstruction. The best.'

Dr Thomas nodded, his expression thoughtful. 'If anyone could do it, he can. But how are we going to get him? He picks his cases—'

'He'll take her. I know he will,' she replied confidently, in the face of their skepticism. In that instant her desire to help Katie overruled her own desire for anonymity. Training her eyes on Gideon, she stated without any equivocation, 'He's my father.'

'He's what?' echoed four of the five voices.

Natalie's gaze didn't waver as she held Katie's hand. 'It's your decision,' she told him.

Gideon didn't hesitate. 'Call him.'

She squeezed Katie's fingers before rushing to the telephone. Please be at home, she thought as she punched the unlisted number from memory. When Harrison answered, she nearly cried with relief.

'Daddy, it's Natalie. I need a special favor. Gideon's

sister was in a car accident and she has a compound fracture of her femur. They don't think they can save her leg. Our orthopedic surgeon is out of town. Can you—?'

'Is Alexander there?' Harrison demanded.

Natalie held the phone out to Gideon. 'He wants to talk to you.' Gideon skirted the table to take it while she resumed her place near Katie's head.

'She's shocky,' he reported into the mouthpiece, 'but no other major injuries. It's broken in at least five places. Our X-rays show a piece lodged against the artery.' He was silent. 'Yeah, we can move her.'

A few seconds later Gideon hung up the phone. 'He's sending an air ambulance from University Hospital. It should be here in thirty minutes.'

Natalie wanted to cry from sheer relief.

The next half an hour passed by in a blur as the ER staff prepared Katie for her flight. No one questioned Natalie's right to remain at the girl's side, holding her hand and whispering words of encouragement.

She held onto the sedated girl even as the blue-suited flight medical team whisked her to the helipad on the east side of the hospital. Just as they were ready to slide her stretcher into the helicopter Natalie pressed a swift kiss to her cheek. 'You're going to be fine, Katie. My dad's going to help you. I'll be there when you wake up, so don't worry.'

Katie gave a drowsy nod.

Gideon bent over her. 'You doing okay, little one?'

'Yeah,' the teen whispered. 'Gideon?'

'I'm right here,' he said, his hand resting on top of hers as it lay across her mid-section.

'Don't let them. . .cut off. . .my leg.'

'Oh, Katie.' His voice shook. 'I can't promise—'

Natalie broke in. '*We* promise,' she said, returning Gideon's glare. She might not know very much about orthopedics, but she did have faith in her father and his ability.

Katie's mouth relaxed. 'Natalie?'

'I'm here, sweetie,' Natalie replied.

'Take care. . .of Gideon. . .for me?' Katie asked.

Tears brimmed in Natalie's eyes as she glanced at Gideon. He was suffering from the same condition. 'I will.'

'We need to go, Doctor,' the flight physician reminded him.

Gideon and Natalie reluctantly released Katie and stepped back to watch the young girl disappear inside the aircraft with its cargo of high-tech equipment.

'Sorry there's no room for you, but don't worry. She'll go straight to OR. Dr Pike's ready and waiting, along with a vascular surgeon.'

The door closed. Natalie, Gideon and the ER personnel watched the special ambulance rise and take off across the night sky, its red lights blinking in the darkness.

'We've got to get there,' Gideon said, heading across the lawn toward the hospital with Natalie in his wake. 'Grab some clothes and let's go. I'll pick you up on the way out of town.'

Natalie nodded, but before she could move, Walter, one of the emergency medical technicians, ran up to them. 'Hey, Doc. My brother has a twin-engine plane. He'll fly you to Denver if you want.'

'Thanks,' Gideon said gratefully.

'He's standing by at the airport. I'll let him know you're on your way.'

Gideon turned to Natalie. 'Meet me as soon as you can.'

Without taking time to reply, Natalie ran through the hospital to the lab, grabbed her purse and dashed to her car. After taking the shortest way home, and pushing the speed limit, she arrived to throw a change of clothes and a few toiletry items into a tote bag. As she scampered to leave she stuffed in Katie's unfinished cross-stitch picture and a bag of thread.

She zoomed toward the airport and parked next to the small terminal building just as Gideon screeched to a stop beside her.

The ticket agent met them at the door and ushered them to the plane waiting on the tarmac. Minutes later, they were airborne.

Natalie watched the lights of the city twinkle in the night sky as they circled Rocky Hills to enter their flight pattern. Beside her, Gideon shuddered and rubbed his eyes.

'She's going to be okay,' she said over the roar of the engine.

He nodded, but his bleak expression, visible in the dimly lit cabin, tore at her heartstrings. His doctor mask had slipped, revealing a family member's anguish. She clutched his hand, feeling the need to lend comfort and receive it in return.

The time passed slowly, each minute seeming to last an hour.

'How did it happen?' she asked in Gideon's ear.

He spoke into hers. 'They were on their way to the football game. Apparently an elderly man ran a stop light and smashed the passenger side of the car. Sara was driving; she has a slight concussion and a few bruises, but Katie caught the brunt of the impact.'

'What about the other guy?'

'He's fine. Hardly a scratch.'

The tension in Gideon was palpable, and she reached up to smooth out a worry line across his brow. Without a word, he swung his arm around to tuck her close. She rested her head against his shoulder, and for the remainder of the short flight, with his warmth and comforting scent enfolding her like a blanket, she was able to keep her worries at bay.

It wasn't long until Gideon stiffened to attention. Pulling out of his embrace, Natalie saw the glow of metropolitan Denver lights illuminating the dark sky like a lighthouse beacon.

'We're here,' she said inanely.

Their plane had barely taxied to a stop before someone flung the door open and steps unfolded.

'Hope she's okay,' Walter's brother shouted from the cockpit.

Gideon waved his thanks before he ushered Natalie outside.

A man in an airline uniform greeted them as soon as their feet hit the tarmac. 'We have a car waiting for you, Dr Alexander.'

Breaking his stride, Gideon said, 'But how—?'

The man grinned. 'Your pilot radioed ahead. It's all taken care of. Good luck to you and your sister.'

Their driver whipped through the traffic like an experienced Indy 500 racer and screeched to the University Hospital's Emergency entrance. The car had barely rolled to a stop before Natalie sprang out of the door.

Gideon dug out his wallet, but the man waved aside the bills. 'Your money's no good, Dr Alexander. Hope everything works out.'

Once inside, a brown-haired security guard strode forward to clasp Gideon's hand. 'Dr Gideon. Sorry to hear about your sister.'

'Thanks, Mike,' he replied, obviously well-acquainted with the man. 'Where is she?'

'Third floor.'

Not as familiar with the hospital as Gideon, Natalie allowed him to lead the way as they hurried through the corridors with her tote bag bumping against her leg. It was amazing how hospitals looked differently, yet they all smelled alike.

They approached the operating-room and met a scrub nurse as she walked through the swinging doors. Gideon grabbed her arm. 'We're looking for Katie Alexander.'

The young woman smiled. 'She's inside. Dr Pike started a few minutes ago. You can either sit in the waiting-room or watch from the observatory, Doctor.'

Gideon rushed to the door marked 'Viewing Area' and bounded up the steps. Following close behind, Natalie found herself in a room directly above the operating suite. Seats arranged in tiered rows surrounded a circular partition in the floor. A dome formed by panes of glass covered the partition, allowing medical students to learn the surgical procedures performed in the sterile area below.

He dropped his duffle bag and sank onto the chair closest to the divider. Natalie slid her bag off her shoulder and sat on his right. Although she'd seen countless operations, she'd never been personally involved with the individual under the knife, and it unsettled her. It was different from watching an unknown person's body being invaded now, when it was someone she loved. Yet if this was where Gideon wanted to be she wouldn't leave him to face the final outcome alone.

She reached for his hand, noticing how cold it was, and gave it a gentle squeeze.

A scrub nurse pointed overhead and one capped and masked person in the throng surrounding the operating-table raised his head. Recognizing her father, in spite of his gear, she waggled her fingers in a wave.

'You made it in good time,' Harrison said over the intercom. 'We're just starting.' As if he knew the question uppermost in their minds, he admitted, 'I'll be honest—I haven't seen too many cases worse than hers.'

Gideon dropped her hand and pressed the speaker button. 'But you can save the leg. Can't you?'

Harrison didn't flinch. 'We'll do everything we can.'

Gideon nodded. Harrison, the vascular surgeon and their assistants bent over a completely draped Katie once again.

The only sound in the amphitheater for a while was the clink of instruments as the specialists performed the tedious process of removing and reassembling bone fragments and repairing the leaky artery.

'I never thanked you for what you did,' Gideon remarked, breaking the relative silence.

'I didn't do anything,' she protested.

'You made it possible for *this*.' Gideon stretched out his arms as he looked around the observatory.

Natalie shrugged. 'I only made a phone call.'

He shook his head, his gaze intent. 'It was more than that. You sacrificed something for Katie. I know how much you wanted anonymity, and you gave it up when you mentioned your father's name. I can't ever repay the favor.'

She touched his wrist. 'I don't expect repayment. Katie is very important to me—like a little sister. I would do anything for her.'

His mouth relaxed into a gentle curve. 'Me too,' he said, covering her hand. 'Me too.'

In that instant, with his dark eyes glistening as he refocused on the drama below them, a realization hit her with the impact of a speeding bus. Her father's motives finally made sense in her heart, rather than in her head. She had done the very thing she'd disdained—called for a special favor to protect Katie from pain and suffering.

She stared down at the surgeon who was painstakingly continuing his task and rested her forearms on the ledge with her hands overlapping. Watching the group's well-orchestrated movements, other facts hit home. Her father hadn't achieved his success totally on his own—it had depended in part on those men and women whose skills complemented his own. Alone, he could accomplish little, but with a well-trained team he could perform miracles.

Her eyes burned. She'd been so foolish all these years, struggling by herself when it hadn't been necessary.

As she contemplated these things an hour ticked by. Finally, at peace with her revelation, she rose out of the chair to stretch and glance at her companion.

Gideon sat immobile. His obvious distress sent a tidal wave of love coursing through her. Moving behind him, she massaged his taut shoulders, gently kneading the knotted muscles until he relaxed and rested his head against her torso.

'How are you doing?' she asked as she rubbed his forehead and temples.

'Fine.'

She knew better. 'Why don't we take a walk? Get something to eat? She's in good hands, and I promise we won't be gone long.'

Gideon's rugged face with its darkening shadow looked undecided. Finally, he nodded.

He followed her to the corridor and they meandered past several waiting-rooms, recovery-rooms and offices. He finally stopped in front of a plate-glass window and stared into the night with his hands in his pockets.

'I remember Katie as a kid. Hell, she still is. She'd never walk if she could run; she was always in a hurry. I don't know what she'll do if—'

Natalie joined him at the window. 'She'll be fine. I'm sure of it.'

Gideon was direct. 'Her leg's bad. I doubt that even your father can save it.'

'My orthopedic knowledge is limited, but my intuition says not to worry.'

'I hope you're right.' He paused. 'I'd better call my brother. He'll want to know what's happening.'

She watched him stride toward a bank of pay telephones and turned to study the city's twinkling lights. The evening had certainly turned out differently than she'd planned.

When he returned they went back to the amphitheater, but Gideon paused on the threshold. 'I want to go in, but I. . .can't. If they aren't successful. . .' His voice died.

'They'll find us in the waiting-room,' Natalie told him. 'It's more comfortable there, anyway.'

He nodded, his face haggard and etched with deep lines, the bump on his nose more pronounced.

For the next few hours they sat in companionable silence. Natalie flipped through magazines without comprehending a word while Gideon drank coffee and alternated between pacing the floor and slumping in an easy chair.

At long last the moment they'd been waiting for arrived. Harrison Pike, his crumpled blue scrub suit darkened with sweat and his face weary with exhaustion, appeared in the doorway.

Natalie caught sight of him and slowly rose, scared to hear the final outcome. Hours of hoping and praying were over. It was time to face the cold, hard truth— whatever it might be. 'Gideon,' she said, to draw his attention.

He looked up. Jumping to his feet as fast as a jack-in-the-box toy, he moved close to Natalie as Harrison approached. Taking her hand, as if needing the same moral support that she did, he asked in a hoarse voice, 'How is she?'

# CHAPTER ELEVEN

A TIRED smile crossed Harrison's face. 'Katie's doing well. Her vital signs are strong.'

'And her leg?'

'We fixed what we could, took a few pieces from the bone bank for what we couldn't, and pinned it together.'

Natalie let out the breath she'd been holding and slumped against Gideon. He flung one arm around her, as if he too needed something or someone to lean on.

Tears of joy brimmed in Natalie's eyes. 'See—what did I tell you?' she told Gideon, sniffling. 'What a fabulous early birthday present for her.'

'It won't be pretty,' Harrison warned. 'And she'll probably walk with a limp—there was a lot of tendon and nerve damage.'

'But she will walk,' Natalie reaffirmed.

Harrison nodded.

The young physician, still clutching Natalie to him, stepped forward and extended his hand to the surgeon. 'I can't thank you enough.'

Harrison smiled. 'It was the least I could do.' His voice became brusque. 'She'll be in Recovery for a few hours, so go to our house and get some rest.'

'Maybe I should stay?' Gideon suggested, his arms still wrapped around Natalie.

'No,' she asserted. 'Katie asked me to take care

of you, and I will. We'll be back first thing in the morning.'

'I suppose you've noticed how stubborn my daughter is?' Harrison said.

Gideon's dimple resurfaced for the first time in hours. 'Yes, sir. I have. Can I see Katie for a few minutes?'

Harrison nodded, apparently recognizing Gideon's need to reassure himself of his sister's condition.

Gideon let go of Natalie and took two steps toward the door before he stopped and turned. He raised one eyebrow in question.

'Go ahead,' she encouraged him. 'I'll wait here.'

The moment he had disappeared from the room, she turned to her father and hugged him. 'I can't thank you enough, Dad.'

'I take it we're on speaking terms now?' he teased.

She grinned. 'I guess so. But I wish you hadn't forced Gideon into coming to Rocky Hills.'

Harrison sighed. 'I'm not particularly proud of my actions either. At the time I was willing to do anything, and I did.'

'After what happened to Katie tonight I understand your motives, even if I still don't agree with your methods.'

'I never meant to hurt you, Natalie. I only wanted someone to be there if you needed help. That's all.'

'What did you send him? That's how I knew; I was with him when your letter came.'

He scratched his head, still covered with the cloth surgical cap. 'I sent a letter of recommendation; the same letter I'd been holding over his head to coerce him into moving to Rocky Hills. I'd had second thoughts, especially after I heard about your part in the discovery about the epidemic. Your mother was right—you don't need my help.' He paused. 'It was hard to admit.'

She smiled at him. 'There are and always will be times when I do need you. Like right now.'

'I can live with that,' Harrison replied. 'Gideon will have to learn the same lesson I did. He's very protective too, if I'm reading him correctly, both toward his sister and you.'

Natalie tugged on her hair. 'I'm not sure he's interested. . .'

Harrison put his arm around his daughter's shoulders. 'He is. Take my word for it. By the way, your mother dropped her car off so you can drive home. I expect you to have things worked out with Gideon by the next time I see you.'

'I'll try,' she said, squeezing his waist.

By the time Gideon reappeared, the lines in his face had begun to soften. 'She looks good,' he said.

Natalie drove to the Pike home on Cedar Park Drive in record time and with little conversation. She'd worked things out with her father, but she still had a few knots between Gideon and herself to untangle. Suddenly she felt uncomfortable. It had been easy to forget their personal problems while they had worried over Katie, but now she was out of danger, and Natalie had to resummon the courage to discuss their situation.

Deciding to deal with their unresolved issues tomorrow, since she was too tired to face the prospect of his feelings being part of a charade, she led the way through the garage to the kitchen entrance.

'I'll show you where you can sleep,' she told him, heading to the staircase just off the living-room.

His next words came without any warning and stopped her in her tracks.

'Everything I told you about myself and us was true. I may have omitted a few things, but I never lied.'

Natalie turned to face him. He stood frozen to a spot on the opposite side of the breakfast bar, tall and sure of himself.

'We can talk about this later,' she began, hoping for a slight reprieve in order to collect her thoughts.

Gideon shook his head. 'This is a perfect time and place.'

Giving in to his polite demand, she dropped her bag. 'Okay.'

'I wanted to tell you why I came to Rocky Hills, but I couldn't. At first it was because of what I thought your dad could do to my career. Then, as we got to know each other, the reasons changed.'

'Oh?'

'Yeah. The news would have totally destroyed your relationship with your parents. I refused to be the bad guy. Life has enough problems to be endured—no one should have to suffer through them without having the emotional support of family.'

'I wish he hadn't forced you to watch over me.' Her voice broke. 'I feel badly—not only because my father stooped to such tactics, but because you didn't get to go where you really wanted.'

'Don't. Harrison already apologized.'

'He did? When?'

'Earlier this week. I called and told him what had happened because I knew you wouldn't.'

Her smile was small. 'You were right.'

'I was only supposed to lend moral support and, if necessary, advice. That's all.'

'And the Endowment Foundation?'

'Max Nelson is a friend of mine, and I called him for information since his father used to be on the board.' Gideon's eyes became pleading. 'I honestly had no idea your father served on the same committee. I should have suspected, but to be honest I didn't think about it. I saw an opportunity to help you and I took it.

'As for you getting the grant because of me, the foundation only supports its medical school graduates. My name had to be mentioned somehow, to make you eligible for consideration, but that's all. Your father even disqualified himself when it came time to make the final decision.'

Natalie didn't doubt his sincerity. 'I believe you,' she replied solemnly. 'But it doesn't matter. Not any more.'

'What? I thought—'

She moved closer to him, skirting the physical obstacle in their path. 'I learned a few lessons tonight. It isn't a sign of weakness to accept help on occasion. Often, more is accomplished when people work together instead of as individuals. If you hadn't taken the initiative I'd still be waiting for the money to develop my department. As you reminded me once, our job is to help our patients, not build up our egos.' She paused to study his face.

'What else did you learn?' Gideon asked hoarsely.

Natalie was solemn as she raised a hand to stroke his whiskery chin. 'No matter what, I love you.'

He caught her hand and pressed her open palm to his face. 'I love you, too. Never, ever doubt it.' His forehead wrinkled. 'Katie will face a long recovery, but I can't abandon her. It will probably put a strain on our relationship. . .'

'We can handle it,' she insisted.

'I also know how important it is for you to be independent, but I've spent nearly my whole life looking after the people I love. I can't promise to just stop.'

'I don't expect you to,' Natalie replied. 'It's part of your character and I respect that. We'll all learn to compromise. With Katie and I banding together, we'll save each other from your overprotectiveness.'

Gideon's dimple appeared. 'Then I have to ask your father for one more favor.'

'Which is?'

His eyes sparkled. 'To add "son-in-law" to my job description. It goes well with the duties he gave me before I moved to Rocky Hills—duties I'm *willing* to take on this time around.'

'No problem,' she reassured him, lifting her chin as he lowered his mouth to hers. 'Absolutely none at all.'

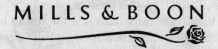

# MILLS & BOON

## MEDICAL ROMANCE

### LOVE ON CALL

**The books for enjoyment this month are:**

| | |
|---|---|
| **A FRESH DIAGNOSIS** | Jessica Matthews |
| **BOUND BY HONOUR** | Josie Metcalfe |
| **UNEXPECTED COMPLICATIONS** | Joanna Neil |
| **CRUISE DOCTOR** | Stella Whitelaw |

### Treats in store!

Watch next month for the following absorbing stories:

| | |
|---|---|
| **AND DAUGHTER MAKES THREE** | Caroline Anderson |
| **A QUESTION OF TRUST** | Maggie Kingsley |
| **THE DISTURBING DR SHELDON** | Elisabeth Scott |
| **CONSULTANT CARE** | Sharon Wirdnam |

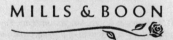

## MILLS & BOON

# Today's Woman

Mills & Boon brings you a new series of seven
fantastic romances by some of your favourite
authors. One for every day of the week in fact
and each featuring a truly wonderful woman
who's story fits the lines of the old rhyme
'Monday's child is...'

Look out for Patricia Wilson's *Coming Home*
in March '96.

Wednesday's child Sophie seems to have the
cares of the world on her shoulders but will
handsome widower Matthew Trevelyan and his
young son Phillip help her find a happy ever
after?

# Fl🌼wer P🌼wer

How would you like to win a year's supply of simply irresistible romances? Well, you can and they're free! Simply unscramble the words below and send the completed puzzle to us by 31st August 1996. The first 5 correct entries picked after the closing date will win a years supply of Temptation novels (four books every month—worth over £100).

| 1 | LTIUP | TULIP |
|---|-----------|-------|
| 2 | FIDLADFO | |
| 3 | ERSO | |
| 4 | AHTNYHCI | |
| 5 | GIBANOE | |
| 6 | NEAPUTI | |
| 7 | YDSIA | |
| 8 | SIIR | |
| 9 | NNAIATCRO | |
| 10 | LDIAAH | |
| 11 | RRSEOIMP | |
| 12 | LEGXFOOV | |
| 13 | OYPPP | |
| 14 | LZEAAA | |
| 15 | COIRDH | |

**Please turn over for details of how to enter** ☞

# Hw t enter

Listed overleaf are 15 jumbled-up names of flowers. All you have to do is unscramble the names and write your answer in the space provided. We've done the first one for you!

When you have found all the words, don't forget to fill in your name and address in the space provided below and pop this page into an envelope (you don't need a stamp) and post it today. Hurry—competition ends 31st August 1996.

**Mills & Boon Flower Puzzle**
**FREEPOST**
**Croydon**
**Surrey**
**CR9 3WZ**

Are you a Reader Service Subscriber?     Yes ❑     No ❑

Ms/Mrs/Miss/Mr _____

Address _____

_____

_____ Postcode _____

One application per household.

COMP396
B

DMA    mps MAILING PREFERENCE SERVICE